To Jul

hooked on

Hooked!

Briony Marshall

BM xo

Copyright © Briony Marshall 2024

All rights reserved. The author asserts their moral right under the Copyright, Designs and Patents Act 1988 to be identified as the author of this work.

Published by TWH Publishing.
www.thewritinghall.co.uk

Except for the quotation of small passages for the purposes of criticism and review, no part of this publication may be reproduced, stored in a retrieval system, or transmitted, in any form or by any means, electronic, mechanical, photocopying, recording or otherwise, except under the terms of the Copyright, Designs and Patent Act 1988 without the prior consent of the publisher above.

ISBN: 978-1-9998669-9-0

For my dad.

Thank you for liking and sharing every post.
#biggestfan

Chapter One

'5...
    4...
        3...
            2...
                1...!'

BOOM!

And just like that, the world erupted.

The same way it did every year at this precise second. Lights, glitter, sound *everywhere*. Champagne, kissing, and the chimes of Big Ben. The promise of fresh starts and the bubbling excitement of new adventures. Friends holding hands, singing a song they'd never bothered to learn the words to. New relationships blossoming over spur of the moment bad decisions, which, from that point on, would always be referred to as, 'That messy New Year when...'

For three young women snuggled up together on their sofa, under crocheted blankets and wearing their softest pyjamas, New Year's Eve wasn't quite so glamourous.

'Happy New Year!' Jemma raised her glass of bubbles to her best friends, who did the same in return.

'Happy New Year!' they repeated.

Eve turned back to the television and saw the

London Eye become veiled in a rainbow of lights. She'd never really understood the fuss around New Year; she was a strong believer that if you wanted to change something, you just did it. You didn't need to wait for the commercialised *'New Year, New Me'* trope. She enjoyed any excuse for a good party just as much as the next person, but she couldn't see why the prices of literally *everything* had to be hiked up for that one night. Even if you managed to get near a dancefloor, you had to take out a small loan to buy a drink and sell your right kidney just to get home.

At 26, Eve was trying to resist becoming a cynic. She'd be lying if she said she hadn't done the New Year nights out and the associated house parties. She'd even, briefly, found romance from a December 31st midnight kiss. But, by this point, adulthood had her in its grasp. Things like bills and the weekly food shop had taken precedence over the treat of a new dress, heels, and a glitzy New Year party to attend.

All that said, she couldn't deny that there was still something magical about the beginning of a new year. Even now, cosied up in her two-bedroom flat with a flute of champers left over from the Christmas alcohol splurge, she definitely felt like there were opportunities in the air.

'Did you know...New Year 2017, I was stood there.' Jemma shuffled over to the TV screen and pointed at the crowd.

Simone rolled her eyes. 'Jem, you tell us *every* year.'

'I know,' she sighed, slumping back down. 'I just like to remind you.'

'Would you say that was your favourite New Year?' Eve asked, topping up Jemma's glass.

Jemma paused. 'The New Year celebrations, yes. The year itself, no.'

An awkward silence fell. Jemma was obviously lost in thought about her university days in London. Eve and Simone exchanged a glance.

Eve cleared her throat. 'How about you, Sim? Favourite New Year's?'

A small smile appeared on Simone's lips and her cheeks flushed. 'Probably last year, where I...' She paused, searching for the right words, '...spent it with Jack.'

'Ew, gross!' Jemma playfully tossed a cushion in her direction.

'Wasn't that the day before you found out he was cheating?' Eve raised an eyebrow.

'Two days before,' she corrected. 'We're all cool now. We're just having fun together, nothing serious.'

Jemma wrinkled her nose. 'Sim, it's been two years! If you want my opinion, all men are dogs, and you should just join me and...'

'You should probably give up Jack,' Eve interrupted.

There was silence. Had they been in a cartoon, the other two's jaws would have hit the floor. Eve knew she was dishing out tough love, but it was what Simone needed to hear. Jemma nodded too.

Eventually Simone found her voice. 'Maybe. But if that's the case, the same stands for Jemma's moping. You can't just pick on me.'

'Hey!' Jemma gasped.

'I suppose,' Eve agreed. 'If it's been two years for Sim, it's been two years for you too.'

'Ladies...' Jemma held her hands up. 'If this is your way of telling me I've outstayed my welcome...'

'Never.' Eve snaked her arm around Jemma's shoulders and pulled her into her hug. 'But maybe you should take our advice. There are other options.'

'You don't even have to go back to London. You can stay here with us and go to Berlington, like we did,' Simone said encouragingly.

'I'm pretty sure you can carry over your grades from your first year,' said Eve.

Jemma chewed her lip. She was still on the

fence, but the fence was swaying.

'I think you should do it,' Eve continued. 'Do some research. They definitely have journalism in their prospectus. I reckon it will be much easier than you think.'

Jemma didn't say anything. She smiled though.

'Eve, am I hearing this right?' Simone smiled. 'Are you giving us New Year resolutions?'

Eve grimaced. 'Oh God. I am, aren't I?'

Simone exchanged a look with Jemma. 'In that case, we've got to give you one!'

'Christ.' Eve plopped down on the other sofa as her two friends huddled together, whispering.

Eve closed her eyes and let snippets of their conversation wash over her. In her mind, she began to dissect the elements of her life she felt the girls might concentrate on. There was her relationship status: single. Or, more accurately, non-existent. She was open to the idea of romance, and she'd done the dating thing. Right now, though, having a man around for more than—as Simone put it, 'a bit of fun'—would mess with the equilibrium...the fragile balance of the flat, and paying the bills, and well, *living*. Then there was her job. Okay, so it had absolutely nothing to do with her degree in photography, but she did get to use some of her creative flair via latte art. And she liked coffee *a lot*. Two very good reasons why being a barista wasn't all that bad. It paid the bills at least.

'Ahem.'

Eve broke away from her thoughts. Her flatmates were perched on the edge of their seats with matching grins. 'We've made our decision,' said Jemma. 'It was a unanimous vote, and one which I think will come as no surprise. It's a challenge we hope you'll accept.'

'What Jem's trying to say,' Simone continued, 'is that we want you to give selling your crochet another shot.'

Eve's eyebrows almost reached her hairline. 'Seriously?'

'It's a no brainer in our eyes. It combines your two passions: crochet and photography.' Simone said this with such ease, like Eve making her dreams a reality was simple. 'Make them pay your bills.'

'How exactly do I do that, Einsteins?'

'You have a degree in one and, well, in the other, you kick ass. I mean, look at this.' Jemma held up one of the blankets they'd been snuggled under. It was a cascade of blues, pinks, and peaches, which were enhanced by the stark contrast of large, black background stitches holding the whole thing together. The pattern had been entitled 'The Summer Garden Blanket'; it was an array of intricate, lacy, floral motifs. But Eve had taken the colourway and made it completely her own. The once pretty, pale, feminine design had become a pop art eye-catcher, which, ever since it had been completed, had found its home on the living room sofa. It was just one of Eve's masterpieces. 'People would happily pay for this, Eve. It's a work of art.'

Eve had thought of monetising her crochet work before. She'd enjoyed taking pictures of her creations; she'd turned her bedroom into a studio, made her laptop her personal office, and created an online crochet blog. She loved that blog—everything from choosing its name to creating its template, to adding monthly content. She'd taken great joy in every aspect of it. Opening an online store to complement it had seemed the next logical step, but sales had been few and far between. She'd never reached the million followers she'd hoped to reach around the globe, and those who did tune into her videos didn't part with their cash. What started as a bit of fun turned into huge pressure to sell. Eventually, Eve went back to posting for fun to dial down the stress. All her dreams of leaving her '9 to 5' at The Bean & Mug to become a full-time crocheter had faded like the steam on a forgotten cup of coffee. But *Hooks and Kisses* still lived on, just as a passion project—nothing serious. Until now, clearly.

'Okay.' There was a slight crack in her voice, but Eve continued. 'Okay, yeah. Sim's giving up Jack, Jem's going back to uni, and I'm giving Hooks and Kisses another shot at glory. Hey, if that's all it takes to get the pair of you back on the straight and narrow, I'm game.'

The three of them suffered a fit of giggles as they enjoyed a group hug. Though none of them wore a fancy frock or had consumed copious amounts of alcohol, they were doing New Year's the right way. They felt like they were on the brink of an adventure.

Their celebrations were interrupted by a buzz on the intercom. 'Who is it?' Jem said, answering the call.

'Hey, it's Jack. I've got a New Year's surprise for Sim, could you buzz me up?' Before Jem had time to protest, Sim clambered over her to push the buzzer.

'SIM!' Eve and Jem cried. She just looked at them sheepishly. Jack knocked on their door and Sim flung it open to reveal Jack, known to some as a respectable lawyer, resplendent in nothing but a dickie bow and a glittery sliver thong.

'Ladies.' He nodded at Eve and Jem then stepped inside the flat and hoisted Sim over his shoulder in a fireman's lift. 'Happy New Year!' he said as he carried her off into her bedroom.

'Sorry, girls!' Sim called out. 'Resolutions start tomorrow, yeah?' The bedroom door was kicked shut.

'Xbox?' Jem offered Eve a controller.

'No, thanks. I've an audiobook I should be getting on with.' Eve stood up to go to her bedroom. 'Won't you need the headset?' She nodded towards Sim's room.

'Fair point.'

'I'll say goodnight then.' Eve lingered in the doorway for a second. 'Happy New Year, Jem.'

'Happy New Year,' Jem responded as she plugged in her headphones. 'And sleep well.'

As soon as Eve closed her bedroom door, she put on her own headphones. She reached under her bed to retrieve her laptop. 'Unfortunately for Sim,' she whispered to herself as she pressed the power button, 'today is already tomorrow...'

1st January 2019

~~New Year, New Start.~~ Happy New Year!

Hey, guys!

I'm not normally one for New Year's resolutions, but I thought this year I'd give it a go. So, here I am declaring to all of you, right here, right now, that I'm going to give this online shop thing another chance.

That's right, welcome to Hooks and Kisses 2.0. *insert party cannon here*

Stay tuned for new content, new photography, and, most importantly, new crochet! New crochet that you'll be able to get your hands on.

That's all for this public service announcement. Feel free to resume your normal New Year shenanigans.

Hooks and Kisses.

Eve xx

(P.S: I'd love to know what your New Year goals are. Let me know in the comments!)

Views: 2
Likes: 0
Comments: 0

Chapter Two

'Hey, everyone! So, today is a very exciting day for me as I have a really big announcement to make, which I know you're all going to love!'

'Oh, God, do you still watch this stuff?' said Jem, seeing Eve glued to her laptop screen in the kitchen.

'Indigo Blue is a goddess!' she replied in a heartbeat. 'She's the keeper of all my inner crochet desires. The creator of the magic thread, the designer of my future wardrobe! She's living the dream, Jem. Living the *dream*.'

Indigo Blue: Internet Crochet Sensation. Originally an indie dyer from the Pickford Valleys, Indigo took to the internet to blog about her daily life from what she referred to as the back of beyond. Nowadays, she had her own YouTube channel that documented her every movement; her own brand of yarn that dropped a range of new shades every season; a blog packed full of PR releases, event schedules and sneak peeks; and an online shop brimming with exclusive pattern designs and branded crochet tools. Even her vivid blue bouffant was a trademark, which filled her TikTok feeds on a daily basis.

Eve adored her.

Peering over Eve's shoulder, Jem wrinkled

her nose. 'Personally, I don't see it, but whatever makes you happy.' Jem reached around and pinched a slice of toast from Eve's plate.

'Hey!' she exclaimed.

Jem interjected before Eve could say another word. 'You know you're capable of all of that, right? And more.' Eve mumbled something inaudible. 'Speaking of which,' Jem continued, 'how's the shop going?'

There was an awkward silence. Eve turned back to her laptop screen. 'How's your uni stuff going?'

Another silence.

'Well, glad we cleared that up,' Jem said, laughing. 'Maybe the three of us should do a rain check on those resolutions.'

Both girls had seen Jack at the flat on more than one occasion that week alone.

Eve changed the subject. 'Where are you off to in such a rush? Isn't this normally your sleeping time?'

Right on cue, Jem let out a gigantic yawn. 'I promised Rosie we'd meet for coffee at ten. It's now nearly half-ten and I'm going to be in a lot of trouble. Something about missing Valentine's Day... Remind me why I do this to myself? I mean, it's not like I forget I work in a nightclub or anything—I've been there two years!'

'Where are you going for coffee?' Eve asked casually, knowing full well what the answer would be.

'Why, are you working today?'

'Do I look like I'm working today?' Eve laughed. 'If that was the case, I'd be in a lot more trouble than you are right now.'

'I was under the impression that managers could walk into work any time they wanted. No?' Jem winked before grabbing her backpack.

'Tony can. *He's* the manager. I'm just his understudy.'

'Yeah, but not really. You've been there almost as long as he has. Right, better scoot. Catch you later.'

With Jemma gone and Simone already at work, Eve finally had the flat to herself. She took a moment to stretch and felt the stress recede. She made herself another coffee and round of toast.

Her plans for the day had been mundane: get some groceries in, tidy the living area, read a little, crochet a little. There was definitely time to set up an online store too...if she wanted to.

As she stirred her coffee, Eve glanced at the paused image of Indigo Blue on her laptop screen. Being a follower of hers now for nearly seven years, she had watched Indigo's life unfold online. She was in awe of the career the woman had built from nothing. She closed the lid of her laptop and took her second breakfast into her bedroom. No more idling, there were things she had to do.

***

A blank page can strike fear into a creative in any sector, and that afternoon proved to be no exception for Eve. The dormant entrepreneur managed to quickly race around the supermarket, she'd tidied the living space in next to no time, and she'd even squeezed in a phone call with her mother over lunch. With two hours to spare until her flatmates were due home, the stage had been set, metaphorically. But all she'd managed to do in that time was create an online store account.

The reality dawned: she had nothing new to photograph or sell. No newly completed projects, nothing new on the hook. She would be promoting the launch of a shop before its products even existed.

Craving inspiration, she turned to the video she'd paused that morning: Indigo Blue's big new project reveal. She returned to where she'd left off, with five minutes remaining. Maybe it was procrastination at its finest, or maybe it would give Eve the inspiration she so badly needed. Either way, she was about to find out. She pressed play.

'So, guys, time for my big announcement. I hope you're sitting down for this one!'

Indigo Blue was mesmerising; she really did know how to work the camera. You didn't feel like you were watching her; she made it feel like you were chatting together—just the two of you, sharing the minutiae of your day over a coffee. She looked so at ease, so carefree and happy, and she also oozed glamour. Eve could only aspire to be the same. She'd never been great in front of the camera; she was definitely better behind it.

Over the years, Indigo had upgraded her filming environment from her run-of-the-mill-spare-room-office into a swanky garden room. Her backdrop was a homage to her success. When the camera rolled, she was always surrounded by her beautiful yarns, accessories, and handmade garments. It just 'worked', and it was a setup Eve could only dream of.

'I'm giving you guys the opportunity to experience life 'Indigo-style'!' The words snapped Eve from her thoughts. 'I'm offering three fabulous viewers the chance to walk in my shoes. They'll complete a series of tasks that will be documented right here on my channel. And, at the end of the process, it'll be down to you guys to vote for your favourite. The winner will get a year's employment contract with Blue HQ, and the opportunity to become the next online crochet superstar!'

Eve couldn't quite believe her ears. She replayed the segment again.

'I'll add the competition's terms and conditions in the description box below. The closing date for entries is February 28th. Best of luck, everyone! I can't wait to connect with you. Ciao for now!'

Eve quickly scrolled to the description box.
Conditions of entry:
- *Entrants must be aged 18 or over*
- *One entry per person. The competition is open worldwide*
- *Entrants must have had an online presence for at least two years and have a confident knowledge of basic crochet*
- *Entrants must grant permission for their image and words to be used by Indigo Blue and her representatives.*

How to enter:

We'd like you to make a five-minute video that introduces you, your love of crochet, and why you think you have what it takes to become the next Indigo Blue! We're looking for real creative flair, heaps of personality and a solid passion for what we do. Please also download and complete the entry form; once completed, email it together with your video to competitions@indigobluecrochet.com. Editing of your video content is preferred but it's not compulsory. Best of luck!

Eve stared at the screen. Video? That would be a completely new medium for her. *A scary new medium.* She immediately countered that with: *how hard can it be? I can learn the technical stuff. And the rest is just talking, right? I can do that. I can talk. I can talk about crochet!*

Excitement bubbled in her gut. She was going to do this. She was going to do something that was completely out of her comfort zone and most unlike her. She was going to put herself 'out there'. Her heart pounded in her ears.

1st February 2019

Indigo Blue's Crochet Superstar Search!

Guys, please tell me you've heard the news!!! Indigo Blue, The Indigo Blue, is on the lookout for the next online crochet superstar…and we've all got a chance!

Click here to watch her announcement video

For those of you who aren't aware, I adore Indigo Blue. She's been my role model for all things crochet for as long as I can remember. I'm honoured to be given the chance to win such an incredible opportunity! (Seriously, if you've never heard of her, I implore you to check her out. *Here, I'll even give you the link to her channel.)*

I'm not sure I've got what it takes to carry such a title. Plus, I've never really been one for video content. But, what the hell, you only get one shot at things sometimes, so I'm going to grab this one tightly, with both hands!

Are you thinking of entering? Let me know in the comments.

Best of luck!

Hooks and Kisses

Eve xx

Views: 10
Likes: 5
Comments: 1

TrueBlue49: It's so exciting, isn't it? I'm definitely going to give it a go. What have we got to lose? Best of luck!

Chapter Three

During her next shift at The Bean & Mug, Eve could think of nothing but her entry.

What am I going to say? What crochet shall I showcase? What am I going to wear? Where am I going to film? Will they like me? Will they think I'm annoying? Will I develop a stutter or a lisp or do something really stupid, like forget my name? Oh my god, who even am I?

She was dragged from her mental frenzy when a tall, slim gentleman came to the counter. He wore thick, black-rimmed glasses and an obnoxiously long knitted scarf...*indoors*! Despite her incredulousness, she couldn't help but admire the craftsmanship that had gone into it.

'Hi, can I get a...' He paused for moment, his cheeks flushing slightly. 'A caramel double-choca-mocha and a large cup of tea, please.'

'Of course.' Eve smiled brightly as she put his order through the till.

'Thanks.' He gave her a small smile and sidled away to the collection station, leaving Eve to her mental anguish.

Between Indigo's announcement and that shift, Eve had managed to sit in front of her camera three times. Her first attempt was relegated to test material after she watched the playback; her second was a little better, but the camera unfortunately picked up noise from the bathroom refurbishment going on in the flat below them. And the third time... Well, Eve felt it best not to even think about the third video. Cue her despair over the whole ordeal.

You could just not enter. The thought loomed in her mind but she shut it down instantly, before it could grow any bigger. It was already February, and Eve felt she was letting the side down with her resolution. This was the perfect excuse to turn that around, big time. This was the opportunity of a lifetime. She couldn't work in a coffee shop forever, something had to change. This could be it!

'Excuse me.' This time it was a small blonde lady, who stared at her expectantly. Eve whizzed through her order and looked at the clock. Two hours until home time. *The videos will just have to wait until then.* She pushed her worries to the back of her mind. She couldn't do anything until her shift was over, and she had customers to serve.

***

'Girls, I have a problem.' Miraculously, Eve had managed to get both her flatmates together at the same time when she got home from work.

'My mum always says a problem shared is a problem halved,' Sim soothed.

'Exactly,' agreed Eve. 'I need your help.'

'Shoot,' Jem said, laying down her controller.

'Right.' Eve took a deep breath. 'You know that I'm entering the Indigo Blue competition?'

Her friends nodded.

'Well, the deadline is in less than 48 hours! And I don't have a single snippet of content.'

There was a pause, then Sim cleared her throat. 'Eve, sweetie, before we continue, I've just got to ask, why are you only wearing one sock?'

Eve looked at her feet. She was wearing one sock. It was a beautiful sock—just the right blend of blue and green tones, woven into very neat rows of double crochet, lining up all the way to the ankle where it transformed into a two-row rib. Perfection.

'I stress-crocheted it earlier.' Eve ran her fingers through her hair. 'When I got in from work, I couldn't settle. No big deal. I'll probably make the other one the next time we talk about diets, or weddings or something...'

The others exchanged a look of concern. Eve didn't have time for a therapy session. 'Anyway, I mean it, I literally have nothing and I'm freaking out! It's all I could think about during my shift. I think I even got some people's orders wrong because I'm so stressed! I want to do it so badly. Well, not badly. You know what I mean.' Tears welled in her eyes.

Sim embraced her. 'Calm down, hun, you've got this.'

'Yeah,' agreed Jem. She went to her bag and pulled out her posh 'journalist' camera. 'And we can help.'

Eve felt relief wash over her like a wave. 'Really?'

'Really.'

'I'll get the rosé.' Sim ran to the kitchen and returned with a bottle and three large glasses. 'Let's get down to business!'

'Thank you,' Eve whispered. She pulled out her pen and notepad.

'You should be cutesy.'

'But not a push over.'

'To seem fun loving.'

'But not ditsy.'

'Show us you've got those crochet skillzzz!'

'But not come across like a know it all.'

Sim and Jem had been going back and forth like this for the best part of an hour. With the volume of wine she'd consumed, Eve was struggling to keep up. Her wrist was aching, her vision was blurry, and she needed a pitstop.

'Guys, guys, slow down. I can't keep up!' Eve hiccupped the last syllable which made all of them laugh.

'I think you should tell them about the time you complimented that guy's knitwear in the nightclub, thinking he was a fellow wool fan, and it turned out his mum had bought it for him from Asda!' Sim giggled.

'Or, or, or...!' Jem chimed in excitedly, '...how about the time your ex caught you crocheting on the loo?' Eve launched one of the sofa cushions at Jem's head. Despite a delayed reaction, Jem managed to dodge the throw and immediately returned the favour. Sim joined in with the cushion pile-on. Eventually, they separated and got to their feet, wiping away tears of laughter.

Jem cleared her throat. 'Tomorrow night, ladies, we shall reconvene. Same time, same place. And that, my friends, shall be when the magic happens!'

Sim let out a snort, which set the three of them off again.

'Oh, Jemma, you are a funny thing.' Sim tossed the cushions back onto the sofa and grabbed her phone. 'I need my bed after all that!'

'Agreed.' Eve suddenly stifled a yawn. 'Night!'

They all departed to their bedrooms. Eve crawled into bed gladly, wrapping the duvet around herself and snuggling into its cosy depths. She wasn't sure whether it was the wine or the endorphins buzzing around her body. Besides all the silliness, she knew they had a masterplan, and she felt her worries lift a little.

Chapter Four

'Hello! I'm Eve, the face behind Hooks and Kisses. I'm 26 and I'm a crochet addict from Berlington, UK.'

'Cut!' Jem called from behind the camera. 'Come on, Eve...bigger! You've got this. Don't be nervous, it's only us.'

Eve nodded and took a deep breath. Jemma was right. If she couldn't present to her two friends, what chance would she have of winning if she actually got through to the final three?

She saw the two girls give her a big thumbs up from behind the camera. It was the confidence boost she needed.

The plan was simple. Eve would sit in front of her favourite crocheted blanket. She'd introduce herself, talk a little about how her love of crochet began, show off a couple of her favourite accessories (making sure to slip at least two Indigo Blue products in there), and finish with a few of her favourite creations. She felt it was the perfect recipe.

At the end of the first run through, the girls huddled together to watch the playback. When it ended, they exchanged excited looks.

'I like, I like!' Eve said, grinning.

'Me too,' agreed Sim.

I have an idea,' Jem added. Eve imagined Jemma in a director's chair and the thought made her smile. 'We could do with some close-up shots of the accessories, so we can flick between macro and micro.'

Both Eve and Sim gave her a confused look.

'Just trust me.' Jem began to reset the scene.

The idea seemed to work quite well until it came to Eve's favourite yarns: Indigo Blue's latest collection, *obviously*.

The idea was for Eve to slowly rotate the hanks to show off the full beauty of their colourways in an intense close-up. When she tried to reposition her fingers, one of the hanks fell from her grasp and tumbled onto the floor.

'Pantyhose!' Eve broke out of character.

'Don't worry,' Sim called, running to her aid. 'We can go again.'

By the third attempt Eve was becoming irritated. 'It's going to get all fluffy,' she said, checking over her hank.

'Maybe we should lie them down on one of your blankets?' Sim suggested.

'Good idea.' Jem gently laid the hanks over Eve's backdrop.

'I have another suggestion,' Sim piped up once the shots had been captured. 'Eve could model her creations.'

'Yes!' said Jemma enthusiastically.

Eve wasn't as confident.

'Come on. I'll help you accessorise.' Sim took Eve's arm excitedly and led her to her bedroom. 'I promise, this will be a breeze.'

'I hope you guys know I'm not a model!' Eve called over her shoulder.

She needn't have worried. With Sim's eye for fashion and Jemma's pose guidance, she smashed it.

'I think, with this energy, we should do one more run of the speech,' said Jemma.

'Okay,' Eve nodded, her spirits lifted. 'I'll give it my best shot.'

Almost effortlessly, Eve finished her speech. All that was left for her to do was smile and wave. 'Byeee!'

'Annnnd CUT!' Jem called, clicking the button on the camera.

'Is that it, have we got it?' Eve asked in a half whisper. She was scared to move, just in case.

Jem looked up from the camera, grinning. 'I think so.'

They gathered round the back of the camera for what felt like the hundredth time that night to watch the playback.

YES!' Eve cheered. 'That's exactly what I was after. Thank you so much!'

'Aw, you're welcome, honey. Glad we could help!' said Sim.

Grinning from ear to ear, Eve reached for the camera, eager to get it sent off to Indigo Blue. But Jem pulled it away. 'I can edit this.'

Eve contemplated this. It was almost 10pm. She'd be cutting it short against the midnight deadline.

'I promise it won't take me long,' Jem insisted, as if reading Eve's mind. 'And I promise you, it will make a huge difference, in the right direction.'

Eve looked at Sim, who raised her hands in the air. 'It's your choice, babe. Go with your gut.'

Eve could see Jem was confident. And she trusted her, 110%. 'Okay. But you've got to give me time to send it. Your deadline is 11:15pm at the latest.'

'Yes, sir!' Jem saluted with a twinkle in her eye. She headed to Eve's bedroom.

Eve felt her stomach lurch. 'Oh, gosh, this so risky. I can't cope! I'm going to be pacing for the next hour at this rate.'

'Netflix?' suggested Sim.

Eve nodded and sunk onto the sofa, thankful for the distraction. She tried her best to switch off her thoughts.

***

At 11.15pm precisely, Jem emerged from Eve's room with a memory stick. The Notebook was only halfway through on the TV, but Simone was already fast asleep on the sofa. Eve dabbed her eyes with the corner of a crochet blanket.

'Done!'

'Oh, Jem, you're a star.' Eve jumped up, took the memory stick, and gave her friend a huge hug.

'Don't thank me yet, you haven't seen it!' Her smug look told Eve she had nothing to worry about.

Alone in her bedroom, on her laptop, her entry form already completed, Eve began adding the attachments. She took a slow, steady breath—this was it! She was about to send one of the biggest emails of her life. She knew to outsiders this would all seem absurd. It was only crochet. But crochet was Eve's dream. This genuinely could be her chance to escape the mundane. With trembling fingers, she plugged the memory stick into her computer and opened Jemma's file. With just enough time to comfortably watch the video, do the upload and send the email before the competition deadline, Eve hit the play button.

To her amazement, it was perfect! Eve welled up at how, between the three of them, they'd managed to capture her on screen just the way she'd wanted. And Jemma was right, the close ups of Eve's crocheted projects both past and present brought an extra depth to the piece she hadn't realised was missing until she saw it.

Just as Eve was about to close the window, a title page flashed up on the screen that read: *Bloopers.*

Wide-eyed, Eve watched in horror as split-second flashes of all her mess ups from the evening flashed before her eyes. From fluffing her speech to dropping her hanks of wool in super slow motion, to moments where she hadn't even realised the camera had been rolling (e.g. when she'd been flamenco dancing with one of her crocheted shawls). *Dammit, Eve, why do you have to be so weird?!*

The bloopers finished; Eve was mortified. She froze for what felt like an age until her adrenaline kicked in. She had to do something.

She ran the video through every piece of editing software she could find. She even tried sending it to her phone and using the apps on there. But it was no use, the price she paid for cutting the video short distorted it in some way, affecting the size, sound or quality. It came out the other side looking awful—nowhere near the quality of Jemma's edit.

Five minutes. Time was running out. She had to decide: crap-quality video or awkward blooper reel?

'I hate you, Jemma Haywood,' Eve grumbled

as she clicked 'send'. She abandoned her laptop and dived under the covers.

***

When Eve woke up, for a split second, she forgot what she'd done. Then she remembered.

Oh. My. God. For what felt like hours, she stared at her bedroom ceiling. Had she done the right thing? Eventually, she got up to make a coffee. *It's no good crying over spilt milk.*

Eve glanced at her laptop on her bed through the open door. Her first instinct was to snatch it up and throw it under the bed, as far from her eyeline as she could, but then she had a better idea. With Sim at work and Jem on a date, Eve had the house to herself. The competition rules specified that she needed to have had an online presence for two years. Maybe there was a way she could redeem her entry.

'Hooks and Kisses to the rescue!' Eve said aloud. She took her laptop and opened up her blog page.

1st March 2019

Allow me to reintroduce myself...

Hey, guys,

With the recent revelations in the New Year and Indigo's competition, I feel it's time I refreshed my 'About Me' post —as a reminder for the people who have been here from the beginning, and for anyone who might be stumbling upon my world for the first time.

I'm a graduate now!

On my last 'personal' update, I was a student. In fact, I think dissertation stress was one of the main factors that led to my last 'about me' (procrastination) post.

However, not long after that everything started falling into place, and I graduated in the September with a first! (I know, I still can't quite believe that myself!) My graduation was a truly wonderful day full of love, joy and success. And I got to flounce around in a cap and gown all day, which made up for all the tears and sleepless nights of student life.

Say hello to Evelyn Brooke Jay, BA Hons in Photography!

I left my job and got a new one

After graduation, it soon became clear that I'd outgrown

my weekend job at the garden centre. It was hard to leave the regulars and the job I'd learned so well, but with my new-found adulthood becoming more expensive by the second, it was time to move on. I'm now a fully-fledged barista, and I love the chilled vibe and downright 'snugglyliness' of my new environment.

I've moved into a flat with my two best friends

Simultaneously, after leaving uni and changing jobs, I also moved out of uni accommodation into our lovely little flat. (The beady-eyed among you may have already spotted this in a few of my more recent photographs.) On the third floor is where we've made our nest, and I couldn't be happier. Honestly, those two ladies are the best friends a girl could ask for! Don't get me wrong, it's definitely a culture shock leaving the safety of the educational system and heading out into the big wide world—but, after eighteen months, I'm pretty settled. Home never felt more homely, and my two roommates are kind, caring, and, above all, super supportive. Put it this way, the flat is covered in crochet, and they don't care!

I've done some paid photography work

It wasn't long after my graduation that the lovely Rebecca from Bekki and Buttons messaged me to ask if I'd shoot her new garments for her new pattern set release. After following Rebecca online from pretty much the beginning, I felt honoured, and I jumped at the chance. It was a fab day meeting Rebecca and being able to see her newest designs. I got to learn a little about pattern creation and, of course, I got to show off Rebecca's works of art in all their glory. Every time I see those photographs I still get an overwhelming sense of pride. Not only did the shots turn out to be exactly what Rebecca envisioned, I also helped someone from my community, and made a real-life friend from an internet one through doing what I enjoy the most in this world. Amazing!

I photographed my cousin's wedding

Speaking of feeling honoured, last summer my cousin married her high school sweetheart, and they asked me to be their wedding photographer. I know, MAJOR BIG DEAL! Their wedding was a small, intimate affair that mainly consisted of very close friends and family. The couple stressed their desire for it to be a chilled, laid-back occasion, but I still took my role very seriously. It was a busy day, but by the end of it, it was worth every second. It passed without a hitch, apart from the intended one, of course! And the happy couple were so pleased with my photos that, to this day, they have a canvas of their favourite shot hung on their living room wall. I'd call that a mission accomplished, wouldn't you?

I photographed my new half-cousin and crocheted copious amounts of baby clothes!

After the success of my wedding photography adventure, when she fell pregnant, my cousin was excited for me to conduct a newborn shoot with her daughter. It was a huge responsibility, but I rose to the challenge. Plus, do you know how many absolutely adorable crochet newborn outfit patterns there are out there?! In that moment my two passions came together, and I was in my element. Honestly, that shoot is my favourite photo collection to date. So cute!

And there we go. Behind all the blankets, cushions, and jumpers on here, there has been a whole other chapter going on too. Let me know what I've missed out on with you guys recently! I bet you've all done some incredible things.

Hooks and Kisses

Eve xx

Views: 51
Likes: 10
Comments: 3

Totallyhooked95: Hey! I love your content. One of my favourite blogs by far. Woohoo! Can't wait to hear what you get up to next.
Bekki&Buttons: You're such a sweetheart! That day was indeed a fabulous one, can't wait to work with you again some time. x
WoolMadEm: Hi, Eve! Wow, you have been busy! I think my main success from recent times is that I've started my own learn-to-crochet classes, which have been a huge success! You'll have to pop by sometime for crochet and a natter. :)

Chapter Five

Friday morning for Eve started like any other. She woke, took a shower, then grabbed some breakfast with the girls, eventually settling in the living room for some 'me time' before work. Simone was chatting away to her mum over the phone in her room and Jemma was already asleep after her night shift, which meant Eve had her favourite room to herself.

Today's activity of choice was Eve's first love: crochet. Eve learned to crochet when she was little, taught by her grandmother. Her nanna said that Eve's mum never had the patience for crochet, but Eve adored it. Many a Saturday afternoon in her youth had been dedicated to learning new stitches and techniques. By the age of seven, she'd managed to crochet one of her nanna's most intricate doily patterns, completely unsupervised. As she grew up, she found crochet to be a hobby that bent and flexed to her developing ideals and changing trends. From black fingerless gloves in her gothic phase to baggy, rainbow teabag hats to complete her boho student look. And even now, with useful foldaway carrier bags, crochet always had the answer.

One of the reasons Eve loved crochet so much was its 'pick up, put down' nature. She could leave a project for weeks—sometimes, even months—and pick it up from exactly where she'd left off. Eve's current project preference was blankets—testing her skills to the limit with ambitious techniques, patterns, and designs. However, she was more than willing to dabble in the clothes and toy department if there was call for it.

Today, she picked up a blanket she was part way through. It was hopefully going to be a Christmas present for her mum. She'd chosen colours that matched her mum's newly decorated bedroom, but the multiple motifs that created the pretty floral design were proving hard work.

She'd just settled back into the pattern when her phone rang. Clutching the hook, wool, and blanket in one hand, with some difficulty, she picked up her mobile. The call was from an unknown number. 'Hello?'

'Hello. Is this Eve Jay?'

'Yes, speaking.'

'Fantastic! Hello, Eve, my name's Andrew Benson. I'm a member of Indigo Blue's team. If I'm not mistaken, I believe you entered our competition.'

Eve felt her grip around her crochet loosen. 'Y-yes, I did.'

'Brilliant, because that's the reason I'm

calling. Eve, I have the absolute pleasure of letting you know you are one of our three finalists! Congratulations! How do you feel?'

The blanket slipped to the floor as she jumped to her feet. 'Oh my gosh! Over the moon! Thank you! Thank you so much.'

Andrew chuckled. 'Aw, fantastic! But honestly, no need to thank me, you won your place fair and square. The content you've produced...well, it's fantastic. I'm elated to welcome you into our world, Eve.'

'Th-thank you,' she stuttered. She reached for her glass on the coffee table and gulped some water to try and eradicate the desert in her mouth.

'What made you stand out from the rest was your gag reel. Our audience just love bloopers!'

She blushed. *Jemma's outtakes! Oh no!*

'It takes a lot of courage to include footage like that. Especially on competition entries. Risky move indeed! You've got guts, I like that.'

Eve breathed a sigh of relief. 'I'm glad you liked them,' she managed. 'I wasn't sure about them myself, right up to the eleventh hour.'

Andrew chuckled again. 'Well, we'll be in touch shortly to introduce you to your mentor. You have Sharon; I'll email you her details now. There's not much more to say other than how great it is to have you on board.

Congratulations again! Speak soon.'

'Thank you, Andrew. Speak soon.' The call ended.

Eve didn't know what to do. Stood in the middle of the living room, she was scared to move because her legs felt like jelly. She wanted to cry out with joy, but she didn't want to worry the girls; instead, she called out to them. Eventually, they both emerged—Sim with her phone against her shoulder and Jem trying her best to stifle a yawn. 'Everything okay?' she asked sleepily.

'Yeah,' Eve nodded enthusiastically. 'That was Indigo's team! I've made the top three!'

Instantly, Sim said, 'Sorry, Mum, I'll have to call you back.' She tossed her phone onto the sofa. Screaming, the girls came together in a hug.

'What did they say exactly?' Sim said when they broke apart. She perched on the edge of the sofa.

Eve turned to Jem. 'That they loved my bloopers.'

'I knew it!' Jemma punched the air. 'See! And you didn't believe me. It's cute, it's real. It made you stand out!'

'That's what he said. He agreed it was a risky strategy, though.' Eve smiled at the sheer pride etched on Jem's face. 'Thank you,' she added. 'I couldn't have done it without you—either of you.' They came together for another hug; this time, tears were shed.

'Well, that got emotional,' said Jem, clearing her throat.

'You're telling me!' Sim agreed, dabbing her eyes with a tissue. 'We've got to do something to celebrate! What do you think? Food? Drinks?'

'I'm definitely up for that,' said Jemma. 'What would you prefer, Eve?'

Eve was about to answer when she caught sight of the clock. 'Oh, crap! I'm late for work. Sorry, guys, I've got to go. We'll decide later, yeah?' Before either of her flatmates could respond, Eve grabbed her bag and ran down the stairs.

***

Eve's day dragged. Her shift at the coffee shop had started at noon; by 5pm she was beginning to wonder if there'd been another ice age during that time. *Maybe everyone inside The Bean & Mug is the last of mankind.* Had the continuation of Earth's civilisation depended upon her and the coffee shop's customers, the human race was destined to die out.

'You can get off now, if you like.' Her manager's voice jolted her from her daydream.

'Huh?'

'You can head home. There's only really clean-up left to do. Anything else the day wants to throw at us, Emma and I can handle it.' Tony smiled at his daughter, Emma, Eve's fellow full-time colleague, who rolled her eyes in response.

Not even Emma Grumpy Pants could spoil Eve's mood. She certainly didn't need telling a third time. In a flash, her apron was off, her coat was on, and she headed for the door.

'Bye!' she called over her shoulder. As soon as she stepped outside, she found Simone and Jemma waiting for her.

'Surprise!' they sang.

'What are you doing here?' Eve said, beaming.

'Did you really think we were going to let something as big as you being the world's next internet sensation go *uncelebrated*? Come on now, girl, we're going out. Out, out.' Sim reiterated the last part with the wagging of a finger.

'Oh, I don't know. Look what I'm wearing!' Eve looked down in horror at her coffee-stained jeans and baggy t-shirt.

'Already sorted.' Sim threw a bag of clothes her way. 'Come on.' She snaked her arm through Eve's, whilst Jem did the same on the other side. 'Let's get your glam on.' They headed for the nearby shopping centre.

After a quick wardrobe change in the centre's loos, Eve was ready to party. Sim had thought of everything—you could tell the woman was a beautician. She'd brought a long-sleeved, slinky maxi dress (with sexy split), a pair of sheer nude tights (just one denier dark enough to hide any visible leg stubble), a bun doughnut, grips and bobbles (to rectify any hair dramas) and Eve's 'comfy heels' (high enough to give the leg formation every woman craves, but low enough that they didn't disfigure your feet). Despite getting ready in such an unglamorous place, Eve felt a million dollars.

To kick-start their evening, the girls headed to their favourite steakhouse on the edge of town. Walking through the doors, the atmosphere was already electric. Luckily, the girls had thought ahead and booked a table; before long, they were seated in a booth, sipping pretentiously named cocktails.

'I've something I want to tell you, before the party gets into full swing,' Sim announced as the waiter left with their food order.

Eve noted the worried look on Sim's face. 'What's wrong, honey?'

Sim fluttered her manicured nails as she tried to hold back tears. 'At the parlour today, I was doing this girl's brows...a routine wax, nothing out of the ordinary. She started chatting to me about this guy she'd started dating.' She paused to take a sip of her drink.

'At first, I thought the guy sounded hunky. Tall, dark, handsome, charming, funny. Then she started talking about all the cute stuff he does—some of them, well, they were a bit personal. I began to get a horrible feeling, so I asked her what he did for job. And guess what? She said he was a lawyer!'

Sim let out a shuddering sob and Jem immediately wrapped an arm around her shoulders. 'It just has to be Jack. Doesn't it? I can't believe he would do this to me again, after everything we've been through! He's seeing someone else.'

Eve shuffled out of the booth to sit on Sim's other side. She took hold of her hand and rubbed it soothingly. 'Honey, you don't need him. I've been saying this for months. He's an arse. Get rid of him. You can do so much better.'

'She's right,' said Jemma. 'Then it's only me not keeping our New Year's resolutions.' Jem's comment was clearly said to make Sim smile, but it made Eve think. Jemma genuinely thought Eve's good news was her opportunity to make her hobby pay the bills. Her friend believed in her. Eve's heart swelled, until she looked back at Sim's mascara-stained cheeks.

'I know, I know,' Sim sniffed. She looked defeated. 'Ladies, it gets worse! In fact, I have a confession to make. Please be kind, I'm fully aware that this is one of the lowest moments of my entire beauty career...'

Over the top of Sim's head, Eve and Jemma exchanged a bemused look.

'After hearing all this, and putting the jigsaw together, I still had one of her brows to do. I don't know what came over me...I mean, I could lose my job...the career I've trained my whole life for. But I couldn't help myself.'

Sim continued to sob. After a few moments, Eve tentatively pressed Sim for more. 'What did you do, babe?'

'I, I, I...' Sim looked up at them sadly. 'I waxed off her eyebrow!' She covered her face in shame.

There was complete silence.

'Er, well...I'm sure she won't notice,' said Jem, trying to reassure her.

'Oh, she did. Almost instantly.' Sim dried her eyes with a napkin. 'She asked me how they looked—and you know I'm a terrible liar. My face always gives me away. She snatched the mirror from my trolley and screamed. She threatened to get me shut down and everything. She was very loud, and quite aggressive...she knocked over my wax stick pot and everything.' Sim wrinkled her nose. 'So unladylike. Definitely not Jack's usual type.' The mention of him brought fresh tears to her eyes.

'What happened then?' Eve asked, in a bid to distract her.

'I waxed off the other one.'

'SIM!' Eve and Jem cried in unison.

'I had to!' Sim waved away their panic with her free hand. 'Because then I was able to micro-blade some back on while she waits for them to grow back. But I'm still a bit of newbie when it comes to micro-blading, so they came out a little wonky. I don't think I'll be seeing her again.'

'Brows are supposed to be sisters, not twins...apparently,' Eve added after a moment or two. 'Honestly, babe, don't stress. You did what any of us would have done in that situation.'

'Really?' Sim said, her eyes glistening.

'Erm...' Eve shot Jemma a look. Jemma looked just as bewildered. 'Sure,' Eve reassured her, as confidently as she could muster.

'Aw, thank you, ladies. I knew you'd understand.'

The food arrived and they all tucked in. Sim soon regained her composure.

Afterwards, they hit the clubs. It wasn't long before drinks, tunes, and chatter were flowing freely. By drink number four Eve was beginning to feel it, but she was having too good a time to stop. With everyone in high spirits, the girls did shots and danced with strangers. At one point, they ended up in a photo booth with a wind machine, which made them all feel a little nauseated.

With all the distractions of the night, Eve didn't once look at her mobile phone, which was buried at the bottom of her bag. She was too busy having a whale of a time to notice it continually vibrating.

Chapter Six

'Shit, shit, shit!' Eve leapt out of bed and began pacing around her room.

There was a small knock at Eve's door then Jem appeared, sporting bed hair and dark circles under her eyes. 'Everything okay?'

Eve flapped her arms frantically. 'While we were out last night I missed five calls from my mentor.' Jem looked confused. 'That Sharon lady. Oh god, I'm going to be in so much trouble!'

'Just call her back?' Jem shrugged. 'It's no big deal.'

'Jem! It's 7 o'clock in the morning, I can't do that!'

'Why not? Weren't they trying to call you outside normal working hours?'

Jem had a good point. Nine o'clock upwards was definitely not the typical business window, especially on a Friday night. But Eve wasn't in the mood to listen to reason. She ushered Jem out of her room, muttering something about how coffee and toast would be nice. As soon as she shut the door, she opened her emails to find a message in her inbox from Sharon Harrison.

Hi, Eve,

My name's Sharon Harrison. I'll be your mentor

during the Indigo Blue Superstar Search. I tried to video call you last night to properly introduce myself, but I couldn't seem to catch you. Is there any way we could rearrange that call for some time today? I find usual business hours rather hectic; however, if you could let me know your availability, I'll see what I can do.
Regards,
S. Harrison

Eve almost kissed her phone. *Phew! A chance to redeem myself!*

She typed her response straightaway.
Hello, Sharon,
Thank you for your email. Please accept my sincerest apologies for missing your call yesterday. I unintentionally spent the evening away from my phone, as you probably gathered.
I would very much like to rearrange our call for any time after 6pm this evening. I hope that time frame can accommodate your no-business hours preference.
I look forward to meeting you properly.
Eve Jay

Eve read and re-read the email around 20 times before sending it. When she did, she instantly got a response.
Fabulous. Expect my call at 6pm.
S. Harrison

***

At 5pm, Eve hit her final stage of nervousness: procrastination. As she waited for the minutes to tick by until 6pm, she reached for the huge bag of wool she kept beside the sofa. Whenever she wanted to start a new project, the stash bag made an appearance.

'What are you making this time?' asked Jem. She knew all too well how Eve was feeling if the stash bag had come out to play.

'I think it's time for a refresh,' said Eve, pointing to a throw that lay across the back of the sofa. 'Especially if it becomes a background for some of my business calls.' She clapped her hands together excitedly before diving into the bag.

'Fair enough. What colours were you thinking?' Jemma leaned over, trying to sneak a peek at Eve's bag.

'Maybe these?' Eve hugged five balls of different coloured wool to her chest—burgundy, mustard, a duck blue, an olive green and a burnt orange.

'Hmmm...' Jem mused. 'They look... nice?'

Eve moved her head from side to side. 'I need to look at them from different angles.' She got up and paced around the coffee table.

The doorbell buzzed and Sim emerged from her bedroom dressed in a short, skin-tight,

Barbie-pink dress and her high, *high* heels.

'Come up,' she whispered huskily into the intercom. Both girls gave disapproving looks.

'That better not be Jack...' Eve started, but Sim raised a finger to her lips.

'Trust me,' she said quietly. 'It's not what it seems.'

'It had better not be,' Eve tried again. Sim scurried over to open the door. In strolled Jack —full of bravado but little remorse.

'Hey, baby! Wow, you look on fire tonight. What's the special occasion?' Jack looked Sim up and down and licked his lips. Eve wanted to be sick.

'Oh, you'll find out,' said Sim, using the same husky voice as before. She took him by the hand and led him into her bedroom.

'Goodnight, ladies!' Jack called over his shoulder, clear excitement in his voice.

Neither Jemma nor Eve replied.

'Ouch! Icy or what?!' he said when they were on the other side of Sim's bedroom door.

'Oh, they're fine,' she muttered, trying to gloss over the situation.

'Not again!' Jem fumed. She reached for her gaming headset. 'Honestly, when will that girl learn?!'

'No idea.' Eve began gathering up her wool. 'Right, I'd better get ready for my call.'

'Oh, yeah.' Jem checked the time on her watch. 'Best of luck! I hope she's nice.'

'Thank you. Me too!'

6pm on the dot, Eve's phone began to ring with Sharon's video call. She took a deep breath to calm herself before answering.

'Hello!' Sharon appeared on the screen.

Eve's first impression of her mentor was that she was a little older than she'd expected. Not that there was anything wrong with that, but to Eve's knowledge, Indigo Blue's fan base was predominantly the younger 'funky' crochet crowd. That said, Sharon was hardly a grandma. Her caramel hair was in a sharp, asymmetrical bob, she wore a cream designer blouse, and her makeup was expertly applied— the most striking part of which was a bright coral lipstick (a colour that Simone had previously confirmed was very 'in season'). On balance, Eve felt it was probably a good thing to have someone older to mentor you if you were a crochet megastar, to help you make more sensible decisions.

'Hi!' Eve smiled. 'Great to finally meet you. Sorry about yesterday.'

'Likewise.' Sharon smiled back. 'And it's fine, no need to worry about that now. So, I thought we could start off by going through what will happen in the competition over the next few days. Then, when the boring-but-important stuff is out the way, we can talk a bit about crochet and get to know each other a little better.'

'Sounds great.'

Conversation flowed easily, which instantly put Eve's nerves at ease. But ten minutes into the call it sounded like a volcano was erupting in the flat.

'Jack, you're never satisfied! It makes me *sick*!' Sim's voice travelled perfectly—it was shrill and high pitched. 'You've got *issues*. You're a commitment-phobe. Well, news flash, Jackie boy, you've just killed this two-and-a-half-year relationship. I promise you...you will never find another woman who will put up with your bullshit half as much as I have!'

The noise got louder and louder. In fact, it sounded like it was right outside Eve's bedroom door.

'What do you expect when I turn up and you're dressed like that? I might have just wanted to come round for a chat.'

'Ha! Like that has ever crossed your mind.'

It was clear that Sharon could hear everything that was going on in the background, though she was trying her best to hide it. Eve saw her wince slightly with every shout and screech.

'What?! I'm not the one stood here in the world's shortest skirt.'

'Oh, and you'd know what that looked like, would you? Tramp!'

'Whore.'

'Pfft. Takes one to know one, honey. At least *I* know the name of everyone I've slept with!'

'Anyway...' Eve laughed awkwardly through gritted teeth.

'Oh, go to hell, Simone.'

'The feeling's mutual. Get out of my flat!'

'Gladly. You're not worth all this hassle.'

'*Hassle*?! Babes, this isn't even the half of it. Go on, run along to your new booty call. I hope you find her wonky brows very arousing!'

There was a couple of doors slammed then silence. To Eve's further horror, her bedroom door opened.

'You know...oh my gosh! I'm so sorry!'

By the time Eve turned her head, she just caught a glimpse of Simone's long, dark hair disappearing back through the door frame. Swivelling back to the laptop, Eve could see Sharon's annoyance written across her face.

'S-sorry about that,' she stammered. She gave a small cough as she racked her brains for something to say—anything that would detract from the situation. *What had they been talking about again? Think, Eve, THINK! Ah, yes!* 'Erm, yes, I believe the response a viewer will have to the words yarn or wool does indeed depend on their location, but also the actual fibre and brand being discussed. In much the same way that a ball and a hank of wool would be considered two very different things within our community. Wouldn't you agree?'

There was a moment of silence, and Eve began to panic that they'd lost connection. *Maybe Sharon had been that shocked by what had just happened she'd exited the call.*

'I think you're onto something there, Eve. In fact, we definitely have a discussion in the making for content already. How fantastic!'

Eve smiled and looked down at her lap for a second, relief washing over her. She'd managed to save it by the skin of her teeth. *Phew*!

'Well, that should just about do for this evening's chat. However, I would like to call in on you again after the video announcement drops, if that's alright? Perhaps we could discuss things somewhere a little more...' Sharon gave a loaded pause, '*private.*'

Eve bit her lip. *So, she hadn't got away with it then.* She nodded.

'Smashing. I'll be in touch. In the meantime, get some crochet on the go for when you have calls. It'll do wonders for your chances when we do the big conference chats. Ciao, darling!'

Then she was gone.

Eve let out a long, steady breath she hadn't realised she'd been holding. A very sheepish Simone peeked round the door.

'Is it safe to come in?' she whispered. She tried to peer at the screen without being seen.

'Uh-huh.' Eve picked at the skin around her fingernails.

'I'm so sorry about that, babes. I truly am. I didn't realise...' Sim trailed off after seeing the disappointment etched across Eve's face.

'You knew I had that call at six. You knew the predicament I was in after missing her calls last night. You knew how nervous I was. Surely all that could have waited until my call was over.'

Sim looked down at her feet. 'Jack came over earlier than I expected,' she mumbled. 'I *am* sorry.' Her apology was completely sincere. 'When I walked in, I'd completely forgotten what was going on with you. I'd never have done that on purpose, you know I wouldn't. I was just upset. I didn't ruin anything, did I? Did she mention anything?'

'She...' Eve noticed that Sim's cheeks were glistening with tears. She didn't want to upset her any further. *Sharon didn't make that big a deal of the situation.* 'She just said she'd call me back. She probably felt a bit awkward, that's all.' She gave Sim a small smile.

'Oh, thank goodness! I thought you were going to say something really bad then.' Sim exhaled, then added, 'I promise I won't let anything like that ever happen again. I want to make it up to you. Let me make you your favourite hot chocolate. And I'd really like to talk to you about what just happened...if you'll listen.'

'Of course,' Eve sighed. 'Go make us a hot chocolate and tell me all about it.'

Sim jumped up from Eve's bed. 'Thank you, honey. Honestly, what would I do without you?!'

'I've absolutely no idea.'

Chapter Seven

On her way to work the next day, Eve received an abrupt email from Sharon:
Eve,
Introduction conference call between you and the other competitors scheduled for 6pm tonight. Please confirm that you're able to attend.
S. Harrison

Quickly, Eve typed out a response.
Hi, Sharon,
Yes, I'll be able to attend that call.
Eve

She clicked 'send' as she reached The Bean & Mug. Putting on her apron in the staff room, she began to speculate what the conference call would be about.

She thought she might have reached a conclusion with one of the coffee shop's regulars. Mr Henson was deaf in both ears, but he didn't mind the company, so he nodded every so often whilst Eve babbled on about Sharon, Indigo Blue, and the upcoming call.

When Tony suddenly appeared behind her, she almost jumped out of her skin. 'How many times do I have to ask you girls to leave your home lives at the door?' he snapped.

'Sorry, Tony.' Eve scurried back to the till.

For a few hours, Eve managed to control her

mental speculation whilst still serving customers. In fact, it wasn't until the end of her shift that she even mentioned it again. Her last task was drying the mugs as Tony cashed up the till.

'I think they're going to set the first task tonight, Tony. It's the only logical explanation.' Eve saw him reach for a large pile of pennies. 'I mean, the only thing putting me off is the suddenness of it all. Surely, they'd have a strict structure when it comes to such tasks?'

Tony pushed the little piles of pennies he'd been counting into one huge pile again.

'The more I talk about it, the more I believe it could be anything.' Eve was about to launch into a list of new theories she'd formed when Tony butted in.

'What if they're cancelling the competition?'

Eve nearly dropped the mug she was drying.

'You know. Maybe they're calling it off completely. Cease and dismiss from the big bosses.' Eve froze in horror, her face colouring. Tony quickly backed up. 'Erm...what do I know? Now I've upset you. Tell you what, I'll do the rest here. Get off home, prepare yourself.'

She didn't see Tony smirk as he turned back to his pennies for the fifth time, having finally achieved some peace and quiet.

***

'Before we upload the announcement video tonight, we thought it only right we bring you all together so we can get the introductions out of the way.' Eve would have punched the air if she wasn't being watched. Video calling wasn't a replacement for meeting up in person, but at least she'd get to see the other finalists. She let out a long breath through her nose. Now she knew her dreams weren't about to come crashing down she could relax. *Introductions? I can handle introductions.*

The screen was divided into four squares containing two men and two women, one of which was Eve. Trying not to be too obvious, Eve took note of the other faces on the screen before her.

Andrew Benson looked exactly how she'd imagined him. Suited and booted, Andrew was a little on the chubby side with dark hair in a sharp crew cut.

'As I'm sure you've deduced, you're our three finalists. I'd like to go round each of you and let you introduce yourselves. Let us know your name and how we might already know you from the crochet world. Inga, why don't you start?'

In the bottom right-hand corner, a petite, blonde girl with piercing blue eyes smiled and waved at her screen. 'Hello, everyone, I'm Inga.

My family originate from Scandinavia, so my passion for crochet comes from my colourful heritage. I'm known online for my intricate Scandi designs via my website 'Inga Loop'.'

'Perfect. Thank you, Inga. We were blown away by Inga's style and the pure beauty of her pieces during the judging stage. It's a pleasure to have you on board.'

'Thank you,' Inga said gracefully.

'Eve?'

She smiled at her audience. 'It's great to finally meet you.' The others nodded in acknowledgment. 'I'm Eve, and I'm the face behind Hooks and Kisses, my crochet blog. My two passions are crochet and photography, and I love blogging because it allows me to practise both. I'm really excited to have been picked for this competition and I'm looking forward to where this new chapter in my crochet adventure will take me.'

'Thank you, Eve. As judges, we found Eve's down to earth nature a breath of fresh air and a personality we feel our viewers will really bond with. It's fabulous to have you with us, Eve.'

'Honoured to be here.' Eve rested back in her chair, glad her moment in the spotlight was over.

'Last, but no means least...Mark, tell us a

little bit about you.'

'Thanks, Andrew.' Mark paused to take a sip of water before putting on a charming smile. 'Hello, ladies. I'm Mark and, as is normally the case in our woolly world, it appears I'm the only male. Don't worry, I always make the most of that.' He winked. 'I'm a huge advocate for getting more men into crocheting and I'm known in the online crochet community for my podcast: 'Has Yarn, Will Crochet'.'

'Thank you, Mark,' said Andrew. 'A man after my own heart. The judges not only liked that Mark identified with that minority, they also enjoyed his choice of media...which is a path along which Indigo Blue is yet to tread. Unchartered lands! We think he'll bring a different viewpoint to the competition.'

'I look forward to it,' Mark grinned. He also rested back in his chair, his mission accomplished.

'And there we have it. You three are the future of Indigo Blue, and we're so excited to see what this competition will bring. We'll be in touch soon, regarding the tasks and getting things started. In the meantime, Indigo Blue's announcement vlog is scheduled for later this evening, so fasten your seatbelts, kids, the ride is about to begin. Over and out.'

Her screen went blank. She dashed into the

living room, grinning from ear to ear. 'They're announcing us tonight!'

'What?' Jemma looked up.

'At the end of the call, Andrew said the video's going live tonight!'

'Aaah!' They scooped Eve up into a group hug.

'I need to cancel my plans,' said Jem, reaching for her mobile phone.

'And we need snacks!' Sim exclaimed. 'Jem, you can help me. Eve, contact us the moment you see anything.'

'Will do.'

For the next couple of hours, Eve couldn't contain her excitement. She refreshed Indigo's YouTube channel every five minutes, just in case they'd changed their minds and started earlier. She put her newest blanket project within reach, but it remained on the coffee table.

'Have we missed anything?' Sim called, as she and Jemma practically fell through the front door.

'No, not yet. Surely it can't be long now though.' Eve's eyes were glued to her phone's screen.

Her friends began packing away their purchases. Suddenly, Eve jumped out of her seat. 'Oh my gosh, it's live! The announcement video is live!' she squealed. 'I'm not sure I can watch it. I feel sick!' She paced the living room.

'Get it on the TV. We all want to see it!' Jem called, her head inside a kitchen cupboard.

'Well, if you insist!'

In seconds, the video was buffering, Simone had grabbed the blankets, and Jem had reappeared from the kitchen with a huge tub of popcorn.

They watched from the edge of their seats as Indigo introduced the competition.

'Here we go!' Sim squealed as Eve appeared on the screen.

'Hi, I'm Eve, the face behind Hooks and Kisses!'

Her flatmates cheered and squeezed her tightly.

'I'm 26 and a photographer-cum-crochet-addict. I love creating beautiful things that I'm able to showcase in my photography. I've always had a creative eye, which I believe is my secret behind choosing such gorgeous colour combos when it comes to my makes.'

'Girl's not wrong,' Simone smiled proudly.

'Hold on a second,' Eve raised a hand to her heart in mock shock. 'Are you, Simone Brown, telling me that I have prime wardrobe coordination?'

'Well, your fashion sense may not always be

perfect, but your colour combos are always bob on.'

Jem cut in. 'I think that's about as good as it's going to get, mate. I'd take the compliment if I were you.'

As the video went on, Eve's phone began vibrating rapidly on the coffee table, to the point where it nearly shuffled its way off the side.

'Geez, you're going to become an overnight sensation at this rate. We're going to have to get you some bodyguards!' Jem laughed as she pushed Eve's phone back from the edge for the fifth time.

'Ooh, I hope they're hunky,' Simone said dreamily.

Eve nudged her playfully in the ribs. 'Jack who?' she sniggered. 'I think you're right. I best go sort my fan mail!' She took her phone and went into the kitchen to address her 'fame'.

'And your notification settings!' Jem called after her. 'Otherwise, you'll be up all night.'

Perched on the breakfast bar, Eve found hidden amongst copious Instagram, Twitter and Facebook notifications an email from Andrew Benson. The title box just read: URGENT. Panicked, she fumbled to open the message.

Eve, where are you?!

Surely you realise this is a fantastic opportunity for a live video. Engage and secure that newfound fan base! You've already hit over 1000 followers in the last hour.
Yours in earnest,
A. Benson

Eve felt a lump form in her throat. *Of course, he's right. What an utterly idiotic oversight. I should be present whilst everything's kicking off!*

She clumsily typed an apology. One paragraph in, she realised that he didn't want an apology, he wanted action. She raced into her bedroom, accidentally slamming the door behind her in her haste.

'Everything okay?' she heard Jem call.

'Can't stop. Busy,' Eve managed to call back as she set up her tripod and frantically battled with her lighting stand.

'Okay,' Jem replied, confusion laced in her voice. 'Let us know if you need us.'

'Mmm,' Eve replied irritably, her lips clamped around a cable whilst she untangled it from the knot she didn't realise had formed.

Eventually, she scrolled through her Instagram for the live button. Her breath hitched a little in her throat when she spotted both Inga and Mark already online. She quickly reminded herself that she wasn't too late. She still had time to save her skin and get in on the action.

A hair fluff and a quick check of her eyeliner and she was live. Instantly, the comments came pouring in from people all over the globe. The feed was moving so quickly, Eve could barely keep up. She was here now, that's all that mattered.

After a few moments, Eve spotted Jem's and Sim's Instagram usernames pop up. She sighed with relief. *They'll understand now. Everything's going to be okay.*

***

When the live was over, Eve flopped back onto her bed and mentally reviewed the last week of her life. Since finding out she was one of the three finalists, all she'd seemed to do was fluff it up time after time. People would give their right arm for the opportunity, but she was making an absolute mess of it and presenting a horrid first impression to Indigo's team. Maybe she wasn't cut out for this after all.

Eventually, she plodded into the living room. Her feet felt heavy, and she was exhausted.

'Aw, you did fab, babe!' Sim exclaimed.

'Yeah,' agreed Jem, 'you smashed it.'

Eve couldn't bring herself to reply. Her head was still reeling with thoughts of failure. Instead, she plonked herself down between her two best friends and burst into tears.

'Hey, hey, hey! What's all this about?' Jem pulled Eve into a hug.

'I'm not cut out for this. I don't think I can do it,' she sobbed into Jem's shoulder.

'Don't be silly.' Sim stroked the back of Eve's hair. 'You've done amazing, and now it's out there for the world to see. They'll want to share your journey with you. You did an amazing job of introducing yourself this evening. I'm super proud of you.'

'Me too,' agreed Jem.

Eve lifted her head. 'You really think so?'

'I know so,' Sim continued. 'You've always been your own worst critic. Babes, you're doing a fantastic job. Just like you said to me the first time I waxed your armpits.'

Eve gave a wry smile. 'Honestly, my pits were smooth for weeks after that.'

'Well, tonight, with your introduction clip and that live video, I think you waxed a lot of armpits.'

'Oh, Jem,' Sim giggled, 'you don't half talk some nonsense.'

Sim headed into the kitchen. 'I'm going to make some hot chocolate. Pop a film on, Jem. Eve, get yourself cosy.' As Jem scrolled through Netflix, Eve did as she was told, pulling out a couple of her blankets from their basket and snuggling underneath them. By the time the opening credits had finished, Eve's fears and anxieties had melted away.

4th March 2019

Thank yous, Friends and Overwhelming Excitement

Oh my gosh, what a whirlwind the last 24 hours have been!

Hello, hello, hello, and welcome to the new faces out there after last night's antics! For those of you who don't know, I can finally reveal that I'm one of the three lucky finalists in the Indigo Blue Superstar Search! Wow, never did I believe I'd be typing that!

Thank you to everyone who's sent messages of support and congratulations. Honestly, without you guys I would never have made it this far!

If you missed last night's announcement, you can watch it on **Indigo's channel** and you can still catch my reaction to it all on my **live video.**

While I'm here, I just want to say a huge thank you to my best friends, roommates, and wonderful support network: Jemma and Simone. This week has been complete mayhem, and your help has definitely not gone unnoticed or unappreciated (even if I have been a Miss Stressy Pants on more than one occasion!).

So, yes, exciting times lay ahead, my friends, and I'm looking forward to taking you all with me on this amazing journey. I have absolutely no idea what I'm getting myself into, but it's so exciting! Obviously, if this leads to radio silence from me, please allow me to apologise in advance.

Also, huge congratulations to my new buddies, Inga and Mark. Let the adventures begin!

Hooks and Kisses
Eve

Views: 10,000
Likes: 7,962
Comments: 5,786

Chapter Seven

Eve woke the next day to an email from Sharon: *Videocall me when you get this.*

Eve got dressed and had set up her tablet before the kettle had boiled.

Sharon didn't waste any time when the call began. 'This is rather delicate to say, but I think, in order to not endanger your chances in this competition, you need to relocate. In your current situation you're so distracted. People would donate their kidneys to be in your position, Eve. And running around caring about everybody else is not the attitude we're looking for.' Her face was stern, her mouth set into a cold, hard line.

'I completely appreciate that, Sharon, and I do understand what you're saying. But my flat is my home. I can have a word with my roommates. I promise that things will change.'

She shook her head. 'We had a board meeting earlier today to discuss the calibre of our contestants—all your strengths, weaknesses, that sort of thing. We unanimously agreed that you have huge potential, but in your current situation, you're not able to explore that to its full extent...and that could be hazardous to your chances. You have too many distractions around you. Do you understand?'

Eve blushed and bit her lip. They hadn't even known her a week yet, how could they possibly foretell what would happen from this point? She sensed that she wouldn't be able to change their mind.

'If you could find a quieter environment to relocate to, just for the length of the competition, we all feel it would benefit you greatly and allow you to focus. I'm sure your friends will understand.'

Annoyingly, Eve realised, Sharon was right. She'd believed the competition would fit around everything else in her life, but she had begun to feel that, to stand any chance, she needed to give it more than that. She had it in her to give more. She nodded glumly.

'I'll give you some time to think about it. Maybe make a few calls?' Sharon was trying to appear sympathetic, but it wasn't working; instead, she looked crumpled—like an omelette. 'Let me know how you get on and if you'll need help with expenses. Please do not hesitate to call me. We really see something in you, you just need to let it run free. Ciao, darling!' Then she was gone.

Eve stared at the blank screen. Part of her brain couldn't take in what she'd just been asked, but another part completely agreed. She reached for her phone.

After her parents divorced, Eve had left home, and she'd vowed never go back. Too many memories had been destroyed. It wasn't the same, being in the family home without her father. One thing was for sure, if Sharon wanted her to enjoy some peace and quiet, there was no point calling her mum. During Eve's final year at uni her mother had found a boyfriend. Jason was only six years older than Eve. Her mum was having a whale of a time and, three years later, their honeymoon period was far from over.

It will only be temporary. It won't be forever.

But still Eve's fingers hovered over her phone. Deep down, she knew what she had to do, but she really didn't want to do it.

Eve loved her dad, very much. And he was a loving father in return. Even after his split from her mother, he did everything in his power to make sure Eve was happy. The end of her parents' marriage had come from her mum, but there was no animosity from her dad. He was a giver, not a taker, but there's only so much you can take from someone before you start to feel guilty—which was why Eve was holding off from picking up the phone and ringing him.

'Hey, Dad.'

'Evie, sweetheart. How are you?'

'I'm fine. You?'

'Same old, same old. How's your competition thing going?'

'Well, actually, that's why I've phoned.'

'Go on...'

'This last week, I've been getting to know my mentor through video calling. And let's just say the flat hasn't been the quietest of environments for that.' Eve coughed awkwardly; she didn't want to go into the details with her dad. 'My mentor asked if there was anywhere else I could stay. It would only be temporary thing,' she added hastily. 'I could be kicked out of the competition next week! The maximum would be about three months.' There was silence on the line. 'Please don't feel obligated to say yes,' she winced. She really did hate calling on her father.

'Evie, I'd love you to. It's been way too long since we had a proper catch up. And if it's space you need, honey, I've got tons of it. Door's open whenever you're ready.'

Eve welled up. 'Thanks, Dad. I owe you one.'

'Anytime, sweetheart. Looking forward to it.'

'I'll go break the news to my roommates then I'll call you with the details. I'm looking forward to spending some time with you, too. It's been too long.'

Eve heard him chuckle. 'You can say that

again.'

'Love you.'

'Love you too, honey.'

'Bye. And thanks again.'

'Don't mention it. Speak soon.'

And just like that, all her problems were solved. Eve packed up her things and headed to The Bean & Mug for her shift. Later that day, as she locked up the coffee shop, she had a feeling deep in her stomach that something was wrong.

**

The next morning, Jemma and Simone found Eve at the breakfast counter rapidly crocheting stress sock number two.

'Oh no, what's happened?' Sim said.

'I couldn't sleep.' Eve kept her eyes on her crochet. *Hook in, yarn over, pull through, repeat.* 'I've got something to tell you guys, and I don't think you're going to like it.'

Jem put her hand over Eve's crochet, forcing her to stop. 'What's up?'

'During my call with Sharon yesterday she kept saying that where I am right now, I'm too distracted. She said I had great potential in this competition but added that I don't have the freedom to explore it.'

'Is this about me?' said Sim, wide eyed. 'Because if it is, I'm so sorry. I mean it, and I promise you it will never happen again.'

'It's not just that. She meant everything—the going out, the not being online when I should be. She says I need more space.'

'If it's space you need, we can do that, can't we, Sim?' Jem rubbed Eve's shoulder reassuringly. 'It's not hard. We can go out, leave you to it.' Sim nodded but she hung her head.

'I said all this. But I don't think it was enough. She wants me to relocate for the duration of the competition. I've phoned my dad...he's said it's okay if I go there.'

'Move out?!' screeched Jem. 'Eve, this is your *home. Our home.* Who does this Sharon think she is, anyway? It's only a bloody competition!'

Eve took a deep breath. That hurt more than she thought it would. 'I know. I think we've all underestimated what I've got myself into. But I do want to give this my best shot. And if this is what it takes, I hope you'll both support me. I mean, it's not like I'm moving out forever. I'm just going on a mini break.'

Jemma slowly nodded in agreement. Simone looked less than impressed, her lower lip jutting out in an unmistakeable pout. *Wow, she's taking this worse than her break up with Jack.*

'If that's what you want,' Sim said eventually,

'I'm not going to stop you.' She hopped down from the breakfast bar and started making her lunch to take to work.

'Maybe we could talk about this later?' Eve sensed the conversation was far from resolved.

'Maybe.' Sim shrugged as she left.

'Don't worry about her, she'll come round,' Jen said gently.

Eve sighed.

'I was going to pop out and spend a couple of hours with Rosie. Will you be alright?'

'Yeah.' Eve stretched, which triggered a huge yawn. 'I should probably take a nap, then I've a few things to do before work.'

'If you're sure.' Jem grabbed a bottle of orange juice from the fridge.

'I'll be fine. Thanks, Jem.'

'Don't mention it,' she smiled as she closed the front door behind her. 'Oh, before I forget!' Her head reappeared around the doorway. 'There's an open evening at Browndales tomorrow night. I asked Rosie to come with me, but she can't. Don't fancy it, do you? Totally understand if you don't want to.'

'Oh, good for you! I'd love to.'

'Thanks, Eve.'

'No worries. Hey, it looks like we're all smashing our New Year's resolutions.'

'Who would have thought it?! Catch you

later.'

As the door closed again Eve put her crochet down and looked around the empty flat. 'Come on, Eve,' she mumbled to herself, 'your stuff isn't going to pack itself.'

***

Around lunchtime, she woke to the sound of the flat door slamming shut. Shuffling out of her bedroom, she was surprised to see Sim's handbag on the sofa. She found her in the kitchen, chomping on a cheese-string.

'Everything okay? I wasn't expecting you home this early,' Eve said, rubbing her eyes. She hadn't managed to catch up on her missed sleep.

'You know I only eat cheese when I'm stressed,' Sim grumbled between bites. 'It's bad for my skin.'

Eve popped the kettle on.

'I couldn't concentrate at work,' Sim continued, her voice laced with irritation. 'Not after our talk this morning. I'm only one missing eyebrow away from being fired. I had to come and sort this out.'

Eve wanted to giggle at that, but one look at Sim's face told her it was no laughing matter. Sim was already ripping open cheese-string number two.

'I can't believe you're abandoning us for a

stupid competition,' she said bluntly.

'I'm not abandoning you, don't be silly. I'm just trying to better my chances. It will all be worth it when I'm a crochet megastar.' Eve tried to lighten the mood.

'They're asking too much of you. It's only been a few days.'

'I know. But they seem pretty on the ball with this stuff, like they know what they're doing. I suppose they're used to adapting to the ever-changing trends of social media.'

'But it's crochet,' Sim practically growled.

'Yeah...' Eve trailed off, confused.

'I know it's your hobby. And honestly, what you do with wool and stuff is incredible. But they're acting like this is a military operation. It's crochet, for crying out loud! It's a bit of fun! So what if you missed a call, or I walked in on a meeting? No one died. There are no children at risk. There's no bomb about to go off!'

There was an awkward silence. Eve could see Sim's point, but that didn't mean it didn't hurt to hear. Okay, she would never earn a knighthood for her crochet efforts, but it brought her so much joy. She thought her friends got that. Apparently not.

'Friends support friends, no matter what,' Sim added.

'You're not being very supportive,' she

countered, unable to stop herself.

'I am, you're just not seeing it right now! I'm talking about the bigger picture. You could put your whole life on hold for this...your job, your home, your friendships. For what? Once you burn those bridges, girl...'

'It's only going to be for a couple of weeks!' Eve replied, exasperated. Sim was letting her feelings get out of hand. 'I'll be back before you even notice I'm gone.'

Sim shook her head as she retrieved her bag. 'A couple of weeks to burn them, a lifetime to repair them.'

'Please don't make this difficult,' Eve pleaded, following her. 'You've just said it's not a big deal.' She winced as the words left her mouth.

'You told me to leave Jack!' Sim rounded. 'At New Year's, this was your idea. Now I'm alone and hurting and I'm trying to figure everything out. I *need* my friends—and you're leaving me. How can I trust you after this?' Tears welled in her eyes.

'Trust me?' Eve was taken aback. 'You know you can always trust me.'

Drying her wet cheeks with the back of her hands, Sim flung her bag over her shoulder and walked to the front door. 'I thought I could. Enjoy your new life,' she said coldly. She slammed it behind her.

Eve remained rooted to the spot, shocked at what had just occurred.

***

Sim avoided Eve for the rest of that day and the one after that. She wouldn't return her calls or texts and she only gave Jem the bare minimum. The night of their argument, she 'stayed with friends'.

The next evening, Eve accompanied an excitable Jemma to Browndales. 'If all goes to plan, I could be working on websites in eighteen months—isn't that fantastic!? I've read that Browndales help third year students get writing jobs, and I got an email from them today...the credits I earned from my last university stint means I don't need to retake the first year. Bonus! Honestly, Eve, I can't thank you and Sim enough. I could have my life back on track in no time.'

Eve mumbled a response. As she looked round the familiar corridors, sadness washed over her.

'Eve, did you hear what I said?'

'Yeah, sorry. It's just...Browndales makes me think of Sim. We made some of my favourite memories here.'

'Oh, Sim's just being Sim. She'll have forgotten all about it in a couple of days. And, if she doesn't...well, in the nicest way possible, you've just got to forget about her. You said you'd hope that we, as friends, would support you. If she can't find it in herself to do that, then she's not being a good friend to you. If you must do this without her, you've got to do it. This could be your break. You can't let Sim get in the way of something like that. Especially over something as insignificant as where you're staying for the next month. Right?'

The girls were outside the lecture room where all the arts subjects were based. Jem waited for Eve to reply, then it hit home. 'Sorry, Jem. I said I'd come here to support you and instead I'm moping around like someone's just died.' She hooked her arm through her friend's. Come on, let's get you in there and into university!'

'That's more like it!'

Through the door, Eve saw a number of familiar faces. As they moved around the room she smiled and waved at various staff members she remembered from her time there. Then she came face to face with the lecturer she'd seen the most during her three years: Mr Clearwater.

'Eve!' he called cheerily. 'Fancy seeing you here! Are you considering post-grad study?' His smile reached from ear to ear.

'Don't tempt me,' Eve laughed. 'I'm here with

my friend. She's considering Journalism here in September.'

'Brilliant! I think Miss Parks is just over at the back there.' Mr Clearwater pointed across the room.

'Thanks!' Jem said, scurrying off in that direction.

'So, Evelyn Jay, what are you up to these days?'

'Well...' Eve stalled. She usually detested that question. But then she realised she had no need to fear it at all. 'Actually, I'm a finalist in a competition to become an internet superstar.' She laughed, unsure how Mr Clearwater would react. To her surprise. he nodded his head.

'Ah, yes, I saw you on whatshername's video...Indie Rainbow or something? My daughter watches her. Crochet and internet mad, that one,' he chuckled. 'Well done. I hear it's a rather prestigious opportunity you've been given there. Rubbing shoulders with the A-listers, my Libby would have me believe. Didn't think you'd still be rattling around these parts with your newfound fame and all!'

'I wouldn't get carried away,' Eve smiled. 'It's great you've heard of it, and I'm honoured to be taking part. There were thousands of applicants from all over the world, apparently. I'm incredibly lucky.' Saying it out loud, Eve felt good about being a finalist for the first time in days.

'There was always something about you. I knew you'd get your break someday. I wish you all the best, wherever that journey takes you.'

'Thank you,' Eve said gratefully.

'I'm in!' Jem was beaming as she reappeared.

'Very nice.' Mr Clearwater smiled warmly at Jemma. 'I hear the journalism programme has had some refinement over the last few years. Churned out some successful reporters, in fact. I believe you've made a fabulous choice, even if I am slightly biased.'

'I love what I've seen so far,' she said. 'I think I'm going to go for it.'

'Well, it looks like our job here is done,' said Mr Clearwater.

Back home, Eve continued packing some last bits and pieces, ready for her 'mini break'. She finally felt confident in her decision. Maybe bumping into Mr Clearwater that evening was the epiphany she'd needed. She could do this. She wanted to do this. She *would* do this.

12th March 2019

#ThrowbackThursday

Hi, guys,

Today, I've been reminiscing. I'm currently going through some massive changes in my life, as you can probably imagine! It's got me thinking about the 'good old times'.

With this in mind, and the fact it's Thursday, I thought I'd share with you my favourite throwback piece from my crochet archive and the memories attached to it. And I'm hoping that you'll share some of yours with me.

When I was at university, I met one of my best friends—Simone. I sat next to her in the canteen one afternoon during Freshers' Week and she was reading the same book as me. We got talking and the rest, as they say, is history. Very early on in our friendship I got the urge to crochet her something. (That's how you know I like you; I'll make you something. It's like a rite of passage in my world. If I really, really like you, you'll get more than one!) Over the years, Sim has accumulated a lot of crocheted gifts; however, it's that first one I want to talk about today.

As the summer rolled into autumn, the nights got longer and there was a definite chill in the air. Sim began complaining about how cold she was. One particularly cold afternoon we had an hour-long debate about how much body heat you lose from the top of your head. That was my eureka moment—I could make Sim a hat! I did nothing but crochet that hat from the moment I hooked my foundation chain to the moment I tied off the slip stitch. My lecturer, Mr Clearwater, even caught me hooking away during one of my seminars and he teased me in front of the whole class. I didn't care, I just wanted to make Simone a hat—and I did, in just under a week. She loved it.

That hat was awesome. It moulded to whatever look you wanted. If you wanted a chic beret, it perched effortlessly on the back of your head. If you were too cold to function properly, it stretched right down over your ears. And, if you wanted to take it with you for weather (or hair) emergencies, it fitted snugly into whatever pocket or corner of a bag you wanted it to. Truly the best hat I've ever made.

I don't know whether it's because I saw Mr Clearwater this evening (my other friend, Jemma, attended an open evening at my old uni, and I went with her for moral support), or whether it's because I feel like Sim needs a bit of warmth right now, but this is one memory that won't leave me alone at the minute. I'm not complaining, it's one of my favourite crochet throwbacks.

There's a moral to this story: sometimes we need to shape who we are in order to progress and grow as people and become who we want to be. Just like Sim's hat, we must stretch and adapt to the different situations we find ourselves in, which is exactly what I feel like I'm doing right now. So, if you see me and I'm a little bit woolly around the edges, I do apologise—I'm just trying to figure out what kind of hat I need to be today.

And that's my crochet themed #throwbackthursday. Please share yours with me in the comments, I love seeing what people have made and the beautiful memories behind them. Isn't it great how your makes can be such a great time capsule for the point in your life in which you made them?

Until next time…
Hooks and Kisses
Eve

Views: 4,000
Likes: 1,531
Comments: 25
TrueBlue49: Still can't believe I commented on your blog just over a month ago and now you're one of Indigo Blue's Superstar Search finalists!!! How's the competition going, have you got any sneaky updates for us?
yarnand_hook: My favourite crochet memory is a shawl I made for my grandma to wear at my wedding. She was 82, and we had an outdoor wedding. She feels the cold so badly now she's older, and she was so worried that she wouldn't be able to last the whole ceremony. When I presented her with the shawl it was like giving her some gold. She loved it, and she's pretty much worn it every day since.
HooksandKisses: @yarnand_hook That is such a lovely crochet throwback. I bet your grandma rocks that shawl too. Beautiful.
More...

Chapter Eight

After moving in with her dad, for a whole week, Eve heard nothing from Indigo Blue or any of her team. She'd done her best to impress... checking in hourly on all the relevant social media platforms, answering people's comments, and posting regular updates about her current crochet projects and her excitement about the Indigo Blue competition. But from the company itself, absolute radio silence. She began to run out of juice.

It was a strange feeling. She felt that she was simultaneously a 26-year-old woman and a 5-year-old-girl in the same body. She believed she'd made the right move, coming back home. Her dad had set up an office for her in the spare bedroom. It had a writing desk, space to film, and one of those funky ring lights. She just wanted an email from Indigo's team to prove it had all been worth it. She kept hitting her inbox's refresh button as her dad made them both boiled eggs with soldiers for breakfast.

'Honestly, sweetheart, relax. When they want you, they'll be biting at your heels. Trust me, I've worked with these kinds of people. They're very good at getting themselves noticed.'

Eve doubted very much that her dad, as a

car mechanic, had dealt with people like them. As he placed her breakfast before her, she appreciated the sentiment.

'What's the worst that could happen? Right now, being part of this competition is dead easy…you haven't got to do anything!' It was a little irritating how relaxed her dad was being about the whole thing.

'Are you serious?!' Eve said, eggy soldier in hand. 'The worst that could happen is they close the competition after deciding it's not going to work, or, even worse, drop me from the running. They may have decided I'm not as good as they thought and they're already searching for my replacement…' She trailed off. She hadn't realised she'd been thinking any of those things before she verbalised them.

'Evie, they're just doing what they do. They'll be in touch when they're re-'

At that very moment, an email landed in her inbox from Andrew Benson.

'Sorry. I wanted to make sure I didn't miss anything.' Eve scooped up her egg, kissed her dad on the cheek, then scurried off to her new office to read the email.

Good morning, Eve!
Hope you're well. I've been loving the content you've been posting about our competition, keeping the buzz alive. Well done! Sorry for the

silence, we've been trying to fine tune some elements for the rest of the competition, and Indigo herself has been a little under the weather—so we had to put the brakes on for a bit. I'm happy to confirm that we've sorted all that now, and Indigo is very eager to meet you all. We're therefore proposing an in-person meeting at our headquarters where we'll tell you all about the first task in the competition.
I've asked Sharon to call you later today with further details.
A. Benson

Oh god... Eve's mind instantly went into meltdown. *What will I wear?!* The temporary wardrobe she'd brought to her dad's flashed before her eyes and she winced. She picked up the phone without thinking and called Sim. But she didn't pick up. After the fourth failed call, Eve put her phone on the desk and opened her wardrobe. *Come on, how hard can it be?*

***

Four hours and a mountain of clothes on the bed later, Eve was wrapping up a video call with Sharon. She'd placed an outfit that included her favourite crocheted jumper on her mannequin.

'So, I'll collect you from the train station around ten, prompt.' Sharon had been all smiles. She clearly approved of Eve's new location.

'Okay.' Eve had nodded, already planning the journey in her head.

'Don't be late,' Sharon had chimed before the call was over.

'10am,' she murmured to herself, taking one last look at her outfit before turning the light off. '10am tomorrow and we'll see if all this has been worth it.'

**

9.48am the next day and Eve dithered outside the train station, fresh out of an awkward phone call with Tony about her abrupt absence at The Bean & Mug. She hoped her day would get better, not worse.

Sharon had said prompt and prompt Eve was. But being prompt gave her way too much time to think. The previous night she'd tried once again to contact Simone, only to get her voicemail. Jem hadn't picked up either, though Eve had a feeling she'd been at work. At 9.59am exactly a sleek black Audi glided into her eyeline, which instantly distracted her from her spiralling anxiety. She watched in awe as a window rolled down to reveal an immaculate Sharon Harrison, who grinned and gestured towards the passenger door.

'Good morning, Eve! Please get in.' She

obliged, suddenly noticing the looks Sharon's car was receiving from some of the morning commuters.

'Right…the plan is, we'll arrive at HQ, I'll get you checked in at the front desk, then we'll head up to the meeting room. Andrew will do his bit, then I believe we'll have the rest of the day to discuss the first task.' Eve felt that, in the flesh, Sharon looked a lot softer. She was still an image of perfection, from her lipstick to the manner in which she spoke. Today, she gave off 'mum boss' vibes rather the ice queen persona Eve had seen previously. 'How are you feeling?' she added, as if reading Eve's thoughts.

'A bit nervous,' Eve replied honestly, 'but excited all the same. I'm really looking forward to getting started.'

'Me too. Last week…all that waiting…torture! I love your jumper, by the way,' she said without taking her eyes off the road.

'Thanks! It's…'

'Summer Fruits. 2017 summer release,' Sharon interrupted, smiling. 'If that's the kind of thing you're producing with our yarn, we've got nothing to worry about.'

Eve looked down at her jumper. It was, to be fair, a showcase of how neatly she could crochet cable, with a petite rib edging the collar and cuffs. But it was the yarn's blend of fruity tones that gave it its true beauty.

It wasn't long before they arrived at Blue HQ. Sharon drove into an underground parking lot. 'Privacy,' she said, answering Eve's quizzical look. 'You'll come to thank us for that. Come on, if we're quick, we might be the first ones in.'

Eve was quickly swept through security in the foyer, who checked her in and gave her a lanyard with her face on it. They then took a lift that opened three floors up. Sharon led her down a long corridor and into a huge boardroom, where a small group of people were already present, much to Sharon's disappointment.

'Dammit,' she heard Sharon mutter. The older woman's suave manner reappeared as people approached, and she began shaking hands and introducing Eve as they went along.

I'm never going to remember all these names. Eve's mind reeled until a small wave from across the room caught her eye. Eve realised it was Inga. As she went towards her, loud whispers punctuated the chatter.

'Indigo's on her way!'

With a hive mentality, the group shifted to create a horseshoe, leaving the three contestants standing.

'I'll be right behind you.' Sharon smiled reassuringly before stepping back.

As Indigo entered the room, Eve felt her heart skip a beat. *I'm finally going to meet Indigo Blue!* Indigo was all smiles and waves; she did not disappoint. Her pastel blue hair was what you noticed first about her. Blow-dried to perfection, with tons of volume and bouncing curls, Indigo's hair was a showstopper in its own right.

'Hi, guys!' she cooed. 'I'm so excited to finally meet you all!'

Besides her was a small blonde girl who barely looked a day over 20. As she followed Indigo, she didn't once look up, her attention focused on the iPad she was carrying.

Indigo headed over to Inga first, who she embraced in a huge hug. Eve could see tears glimmer on Inga's cheeks. *I totally feel you, Inga. I hope I can hold it together.*

Next, Indigo went to Mark. Eve took a moment to take in what she was wearing, which was a full length, tiered dress with a cosmic pattern—galaxies, moons, planets, and twinkling stars. Over the dress, she wore a long crocheted cardigan. The yarn was from Indigo's space-themed collection from last November, but Eve had never seen the pattern before. The back panel had a central planet motif with rings circling out in a beautiful midnight blue mixed with purple tones. The addition of some small crystal beads weaved throughout the piece took its beauty to another realm. By the time Eve had finished processing it, Indigo stood before her.

'And you must be Eve. Hello, honey! So lovely to meet you. I've heard some incredible things about your blog! I look forward to seeing what you come up with in this competition.'

Indigo Blue knows my name! Indigo Blue knows about my blog! Had the world ended right there and then, Eve would have died happy.

'T-thank you,' Eve managed, completely starstruck and unable to hide it, regardless of her vow. 'I plan to give it my all.' Indigo gave her a hug. It was such a warm, welcoming embrace that Eve completely understood why Inga had a shed a few tears.

'Right then!' Andrew Benson bellowed. 'Now all the pleasantries are out of the way, let's get down to business.'

Everyone fell silent as Andrew worked the room with expertise. He managed to make eye contact with everyone in the room as he spoke.

'Inga, Mark, Eve...Emily will furnish you all with a tablet. On it is the contract for this competition that I would like you to sign before we continue. You can read it, by all means, but I must emphasise that, if you do not sign it, you will lose your place in this competition. We run a well-oiled machine here, and our business secrets must be kept private for us to thrive. A failure to keep private the sensitive information you may become privy to during your time in this competition could be lethal for us. We therefore ask everyone who visits our office to sign a secrecy oath, which is, in essence, what you're signing now.'

Emily presented Eve with a tablet. Coyly, she scrolled through the document. *There seems to be a lot of words here for that one clause.* She caught Emily giving her a cold look, so she promptly put her head back down and scribbled her signature in the box.

'Emily, do we have all three signatures?' Emily nodded.

'Splendid! Thank you all for your co-operation.' Again, Andrew scanned the room before continuing. 'So, the outline for our competition is as follows. The competition will run for the next three months, leading us perfectly to the launch of Indigo's summer yarn collection. Fantastic marketing idea...well done, Josie. Where are you?'

A young brunette girl with large, tortoiseshell-rimmed glasses waved her hand.

'Here, Andrew!' she squeaked from the back of the room.

'Fantastic idea! Honestly, everyone, we've got to watch that one!' He cleared his throat. 'Sorry, I digress. During those three months, we'll be setting you a series of tasks to complete. They will all in some way test your calibre, to see if you have what it takes to make it in this industry.' Eve gulped—she thought she'd signed up for a crochet competition, not the military. The thought stung as Sim's words came back to her, but she did her best to brush them aside. 'I promise you, it's in no way as easy as our wonderful Indigo here makes it seem.' Andrew paused to let the focus drift to Indigo. She smiled politely at the compliment but waved the attention away. 'Your tasks will then be shared across our various online platforms for our audience to judge. Each task will have a winner picked by us and a winner picked by our audience. This could be the same person or two different ones, only time will tell. All three of you will continue competing against each other until the very last second. We'll announce the overall winner during the live launch of Indigo's new range. I'm sure, by that point, we'll have a much clearer idea of who that winner should be.' Eve saw Mark's mentor, Janet, give him a discreet nudge. Mark's grin widened.

'Do we all understand?' There was a mumble of agreeance from the three contestants. 'Jolly good! So, on to your first task. We're looking for *relatable*. First impressions always count, and if you're going to be the next crochet superstar, you need to start making friends and getting people to like you from the get-go. Nobody likes to say it, but much of the online world is a popularity contest.' A ripple of false laughter travelled across the room.

'We want you each to write a blog that Indigo's fans will connect with,' Andrew continued. 'It must be a minimum of 1,000 words and include photographs. I expect your entry for this task to be completed and submitted to me one week today at the latest.'

'I'm sure that will play entirely to your strengths,' Sharon murmured in her ear. 'I have every faith in you. You have the advantage. I'm pretty sure we can get a strong lead here.' She put a hand on Eve's arm. 'As long as you don't have any more distractions.'

'I promise you, there won't be,' Eve whispered back.

Andrew had more to say. 'I urge you to take the rest of this afternoon to talk with your mentors and nail the foundations of your first task. I've reserved you each a meeting pod just along the corridor. Use your time together wisely, and I look forward to reading what you all come up with.' Andrew nodded and a spatter of applause came forth.

People began to leave, and Sharon led Eve to their booth. 'Come on, time to get down to business.' Eve looked over her shoulder for Indigo, but it appeared she'd already left.

***

'Eve, you're a natural at this,' said Sharon, pushing her notebook aside. 'I'm pretty sure there's a week's worth of ideas there that you've come up with in just a couple of hours.'

The pod was only comfortable for two people. It had a small desk, and it was sectioned off from the rest of the world for privacy. Because she'd been able to concentrate, Eve had channelled her creativity and come up with the blog topics in next to no time.

'I think our work here is done,' said Sharon as she stretched out. 'I'm happy with your ideas. I think we're onto a winner. All I have to say is...crack on.'

Eve couldn't help but grin. 'You really think so?'

'Definitely.' Sharon tucked her chair in and reached for her coat. 'Oh, one last thing.' She lowered her voice. 'Once we leave the pod, don't mention any of your ideas out loud. To anyone.

Walls have ears.'

Eve nodded and mimed the zipping of her lips, which made Sharon smile. 'Honestly, competitions like this can get nasty. You have to watch yourself, even if you think someone's a friend.'

Heading back to Sharon's car, Eve felt far from defensive or surreptitious; in fact, she felt as though she'd made a breakthrough. Prickly Sharon had turned out to be an appreciative mentor and a much-needed ally in this competition and amongst the craziness of the internet. And Eve had also met one of her idols. She felt like she was walking on cloud nine.

Chapter Nine

Eve learned very quickly that having nothing but a clock ticking away in an otherwise silent room could be deafening. She was on the third day of the blog writing task and the creative juices that had flowed on Friday seemed to have dried up over the weekend. It was now Monday and Eve had exactly three hours before her shift started. Her dad was at work, and she had none of her usual home comforts or projects to tinker with as distractions. The more she stared at her computer screen, the less the words came.

'Relatable, relatable, relatable,' Eve muttered her new mantra over and over. She'd correlated her notes from her personal crochet journey into a list for her research. Now, she sat in front of her title: The Crocheter's To-Do List. An hour had passed already, and inspiration just would not come.

With a big sigh, Eve was about to switch off her laptop to investigate her dad's fridge when a little bubble popped up at the bottom of her screen.

How's it going?

Eve clicked on the Facebook message and recognised Inga's face in the thumbnail image.

The walls have ears. Sharon's words came

into Eve's mind.

'All good, thank you,' Eve lied through her teeth. 'You?'

Inga's response was immediate. 'Good, good. I'm struggling to find a way to get into it, but I think I've got my idea. Fancy a coffee break?'

Eve's fingers hovered over the keyboard. Was this the right move to make? She would usually jump at the chance of a chat over a coffee with anyone, and she really would love to learn more about Inga. Going through something like this but remaining complete strangers felt wrong somehow—even though they were technically 'rivals' (at least, that's how the competition had orchestrated things). If she accepted, would she be breaking some unwritten rule? Would she be penalised for doing so? Would she regret it? But surely Inga was taking the same risk? She'd also be breaking the code of conduct, if such a thing existed.

Another messaged appeared on screen: *We won't talk about the competition, I promise. It would just be nice to get to know you. I feel like they're trying to keep us separate and I kind of hate that.*

A couple of seconds later, she added: *I'm all for 'let's be friends' but also for 'let the best man (or woman!) win' – so it's cool if you don't want to, honestly.*

That made her mind up. She typed: *I'd love to. But don't we live miles apart?* She leaned back in her chair and waited for Inga's response.

I'm renting an apartment for the duration of the competition. I think I'm only a 20-minute train ride from you.

Eve raised an eyebrow at this. Intrigue was definitely getting the better of her. *I work at The Bean & Mug in Berlington. I've got a few hours before my shift starts—I could meet you there?*

Deal. See you there in an hour?

See you then. Eve added a grinning emoji.

Inga's status switched to 'offline'.

'I'd better get a move on,' Eve said to herself. She closed down her laptop and grabbed her coat. Leaving the house, she felt her stomach flip. *I hope I've made the right decision.*

***

As Eve opened the door to The Bean & Mug, she couldn't believe her eyes. She found Inga in the crowd instantly, because her eyes had been drawn to the person sitting opposite her, the person with the pale blue hair. For a moment, Eve was rooted to the spot. Indigo Blue, *the* Indigo Blue, was having a coffee in The Bean & Mug. She wove her way through the other customers to their table.

'Sorry for not mentioning Indigo before,' Inga jumped up as soon as Eve approached to give her a hug. 'I thought you might have been a bit weirded out if I'd opened with that.'

'Please, sit.' Indigo pulled out the chair next to her. 'I'll get you a drink. What would you like?'

'Cappuccino, please,' she said in a daze as Indigo went to the counter.

'Are you okay?' Inga asked, concern on her face.

'Oh, yes. I just wasn't expecting that.'

'Of course,' Inga nodded. 'There's method in our madness.'

Indigo returned with Eve's cappuccino.

Inga took a deep breath. 'I'm just going to get this out of the way, so we can all have a nice coffee and a chat.'

Indigo nodded. Eve noted how different she looked. Her trademark hair was pulled back into a low ponytail, and she wasn't wearing a scrap of makeup. In fact, if it wasn't for the hair, she may have struggled to recognise her.

'Indigo and I are friends,' Inga began, 'outside of the competition. We've been talking online for years.'

'When we launched the competition,' Indigo continued, 'I invited Inga to be one of my finalists. I've always admired her talent, and it gave us a way to spend some time with each other.'

'But ever since I got here, they've been trying to keep us apart. Honestly, I met Indigo in the flesh for the first time when you did, Eve, it's crazy. It's probably why I got so emotional.'

Indigo patted Inga's arm.

'I want to make it clear that my friendship with Indigo gives me no advantage whatsoever in this competition.' Inga said in earnest.

'Unfortunately, my influence doesn't hold much bearing these days,' said Indigo ruefully. 'In case you hadn't noticed already. Plus, the majority of the competition, I believe, will be down to the public vote. My team are always trying to figure out what speaks most to my audience. I just wish they'd actually let me interact with you guys. Since you three have arrived they've become even stricter.'

Eve nodded and finally felt steadied enough to take a sip of her coffee. 'Strict seems an understatement.'

'See.' Indigo threw her hands up in frustration. 'Honestly, they've gone so military. I can only apologise.'

'What about Mark?' asked Eve. 'Does he know this too?'

Inga shook her head. 'I tried to contact him today, in the same way I reached out to you. But he didn't respond.'

'Definitely a closed book, that one,' said

Indigo.

Inga smiled brightly. 'I so hoped you'd meet us today. I wanted you to be part of our crochet gang! The moment I saw you on the conference call, I knew you were one of us. I couldn't wait to meet you.'

'Oh god, yes!' Indigo clapped her hands. 'I *loved* your competition entry. You're a natural in front of the camera—and behind it, too!'

Eve would never have believed what she'd done that day...talking to Indigo Blue about all things crochet before her shift. The three of them got on like a house on fire. It was a shame they were being kept apart for reasons none of them knew. Within a couple of hours, they'd covered everything from current projects and personal crochet disasters to their favourite yarn, favourite hooks, and favourite designers (when Eve said Indigo and emphasised that this was a genuine choice, the influencer went as red as a beetroot).

By the time Eve put on her apron, she was dying to write the blog post she'd been dithering over.

'See you soon,' said Inga as the pair got ready to leave. 'I hope we get to do this again soon.'

'Me too,' said Eve, hugging Inga goodbye.

'I've had a fabulous afternoon,' Indigo beamed, hugging Eve in turn. 'Good luck with the blog post, honey. You'll absolutely smash it!'

After they'd left, she collected their empty mugs and took them into the kitchen. Nothing could deflate her mood that afternoon, not even two customer complaints and an empty tip jar.

***

Her usual routine after a shift at work was to get home, jump in the shower, get snuggled in her cosy pyjamas and watch telly until it was time for bed (residing at her father's changed nothing). That night, as soon as she got back, she ran straight to her new office and opened up her laptop.

'Would you like any dinner, sweetheart?' her dad called from the kitchen.

'Leave mine in the oven, please,' she called back, 'I won't be long.' Her fingers couldn't type fast enough as she extracted all the ideas floating around her head.

20th March 2019

The Crocheter's To-Do List - and why it's necessary

Hey, guys! It's Eve here, blogging on behalf of Indigo Blue. Today, I want to talk to you about a crocheter's worst kept secret. The monster under the bed. The elephant currently sat in craft rooms the world over! I'm talking about **The To-Do List!**

I know many of you may have cowered away from the screen in terror at the mere mention of those words. It's okay, you can come back. It's a safe space here, there's no need to shy away. We're going to get our dirty laundry out in the open today, together! I promise, by the end of this, you'll feel much better. And for those of you lucky enough to not have the foggiest idea of what I'm talking about, let me lay it down for you. Hey, who knows, you might be in this club without even realising it! #buddies

As any crafter will know (this phenomenon is not restricted to crochet!), once you get a feel for your craft, the need to experiment and strengthen your skill takes hold. Soon enough, you find all manner of projects that can stretch your ability in a variety of ways. You're on this exciting adventure, and suddenly, the thrill of the ride is the only high you need. You're dabbling in bits and pieces left, right, and centre, and *loving* it! Of course your other half would adore a pair of knitted socks for Valentine's Day. Yes, Auntie Maud would look fabulous in a crocheted cable jumper. Obviously, no dog bed is complete without a graphghan blanket! And there's nothing quite like Christmas without an amigurumi elf. Wait! What? I can spin my own yarn…?!

But what this means, for the crochet-inclined at least, is mountains of wool and hooks invading your personal space—properly moving in and setting up camp. And yet you invite more and more into your home. You can never fully scratch that itch. What evolves is a never-ending list of projects you know you need to finish (or, in some extreme cases, start!). Thus, is born **The To- Do List.**

I've heard it called many things in my time as a crocheter: WIPS, UFOs, stash, body bags, the graveyard. In essence, they all boil down to the same (ongoing) queue that you never quite see the end of.

My To-Do List took shape when I was young, almost straight after my first successful granny square! Over the years, my response to it has varied.

At first, it was exciting to create a list of colourful things I was going to bring into existence using my own bare hands. Anything my friends or family could think of, I could crochet it. As the requests came flooding in, the list grew longer and longer and the excitement to make them all and see the joy on other people's faces was euphoric! Throughout my teens, my list brought calm and control when everything else in my life felt like it was going off the rails. Making a physical list of projects I wanted to make brought a welcome sense of organisation and forward planning.

I tried to use my To-Do List as the reason why I shouldn't buy more yarn. I typed it up on my phone and showered it with emojis. I hoped that the fear and panic of a never-ending To-Do List, right there, staring me in the face, would be enough to halt crochet-related spending. But it didn't. Then there's the shame. The embarrassment of having a list of unfinished projects so long that you can't remember them all. I'm talking about lists so long they no longer fit on a single side of notepaper!

And the blushing that same To Do List evokes when the cashier at the craft shop remembers a project you bought the supplies for over three months ago and they ask you how it turned out…and you don't even remember it, let alone have any updates to share. The shame! The guilt! The embarrassment!

My most recent emotional state regarding this topic, and the reason why I started this blog post in the first place, is that we should be embracing our To-Do Lists, not shunning them!

During the last couple of years, I've learned to love my To-Do List. After all, it's the blueprint of my future successes. It's not something I should fear; it's a path to guide me through improvement, continuation and success…all of which I will come to conquer.

The truth: we all have one of these lists, whether we like to admit it or not. It's one of the things that makes us all part of the same gang. It may come under different names or guises; some may be physical, some digital.

And I know, I know, it can be an embarrassment, a shop blocker, a shaming tool used frivolously by our loved ones, but hopefully, I've shown you that it doesn't have to be that way.

These lists pay homage to our craft. They're a pledge to yourself. An achievements list. A promise. Your own personal Everest.

To conclude this post, I thought I'd share my **Current To-Do List**, and I encourage you to share yours in the comments. Let's conquer Everest together!

Hooks and Kisses
Eve xx

Eve's Current Crochet To-Do List:
- Socks for all the family (this year's crafty Christmas gift: SORTED. Potentially all matching, too. It's cute, and it saves on wool costs)
- Summer dress for baby Belle (may need to purchase more yarn, babies do grow fast)
- Ugly Christmas jumper (because no crocheter's wardrobe is complete without one)
- Basic crochet tee (the everyday staple, except this one's crocheted)
- Lacy shawl (does anyone actually wear these once they finish them? That said, they're SO beautiful—I must make one. Maybe someone I know will get married soon so I have a more legitimate excuse. The yarn was so delicate and feminine, I just couldn't resist)

- Intricate multi-coloured blanket (I swear this began life as a crochet-a-long, but I fell so far behind I gave up and stored it away for a rainy day. It will see the light of day again! It's just that all the fun goes when people are running off ahead, showing off without you. You kind of lose your mojo)
- Am-me-gurumi 'me' doll (I couldn't resist such a fantastic pun, and who wouldn't want a pocket-sized version of themselves?)
- Obscure pieces of home furnishings that do not need to be made (I'll be honest, this is just one heading to scale down this list. In my original version, this reads: wall hanging, rug, futon, bean bag. I repeat, none of these things need to be crocheted, but they could be)
- Crochet bikini (why not? It will be a super quick project. Most likely a stash buster, in fact. I just need to remember that I shouldn't wear it if I'm going swimming—that could be a disaster)
- Pastel granny square (when does a crocheter not have a granny square on a hook somewhere? Plus, I've been told, if I keep going for long enough, I can just sew the corners together and I'll have made myself a snazzy little cocoon shrug with almost zero effort. Win/win)
- Fibre that I need to finish spinning (this is so I can create something and get double the satisfaction of making whatever it is with my bare hands)

Chapter Ten

'It's just a To-Do List. I could have done that and mine would have probably been twice as long,' Mark snarled.

It was the second group meet up. The results of the first task had just been announced and the second task was about to be set. Across the room, Eve and Inga exchanged a glance.

'Exactly, it was *relatable*. Eve's blog perfectly fitted the brief, that's why she wins our vote for this round.' Emily pursed her lips tightly.

'But everyone makes mistakes! I was exposing my vulnerability,' Mark whined.

'Not everyone likes to be reminded of their flaws without compassion. Eve exposed insecurity, but empowered us, and the public for that matter. She stormed the audience vote too. The next task is about to be announced—maybe you'll be luckier with that one?'

Oof! She takes no prisoners!

In Andrew Benson's absence, Emily, the small, mute blonde girl, who Eve had presumed was Indigo's secretary, was introducing the next part of the challenge.

Eve had taken the time to read both of the other contestants' blogs. She'd have read Inga's anyway, out of genuine interest. But she also wanted to understand Mark's vibe and learn more about him. Whether he knew it or not, his true colours were becoming apparent.

'Without further ado, I'd like to announce the second task. You've got two weeks to shoot and edit a vlog. We'll be sending you all on a day trip to try your hands at hand-dyeing some yarn. We want each of you to take a camera along and to create a video diary of your experience. You'll then have a week to compile your footage and edit it. We'll review your entries before uploading them to Indigo's YouTube channel. Again, we shall award a point to the vlog that we believe to be the best, and the public will again cast their vote. If you have any questions, please discuss these with your mentor. Good luck, and happy vlogging!'

Briskly, Emily walked over to Indigo, who was sat in the corner, and whispered something in her ear. They all got ready to leave. As Indigo passed, she made sure to catch Eve's eye and mouthed 'good luck'.

'So, how much do you know about yarn dyeing?' asked Sharon as they left the room.

***

It turned out that Eve didn't know anything about yarn dyeing. She'd never been to a yarn-dyeing class before, or a wool farm for that matter. When she stepped out of the taxi onto the crisp gravel path, her jaw hit the floor.

It was a beautiful day in the middle of April, the sun shining brightly over the lush landscape. Meadow after meadow spread out before her, leading to a backdrop of grassy hills, mountains, and blue skies. Eve spotted some animal pens and, in the centre of everything was a cottage, complete with smoking chimney. It was the definition of picturesque.

They were visiting 'Lofties. One of Indigo's best friends just happened to run a farm full of sheep and alpacas and she spun their coats into yarn. Eve had watched many a video shot here as an Indigo Blue fan but seeing it in the flesh made her realise how little was actually captured with a camera lens.

'Hi!' A woman approached, who she assumed was who they were meant to be meeting. 'You must be Eve,' she said.

'And you must be Kate.' She gave her the warmest of hugs.

'You're the first one here. Feel free to take a look around...maybe get a bit of cheeky footage before anyone else.' Kate smiled before heading towards another car that had just arrived.

Seizing the opportunity, Eve pulled out the camera the Indigo Blue team had loaned her. It was a swanky piece of kit, and she was scared of dropping it. She knew she wouldn't be able to afford to replace it.

Holding the camera high, she clicked the button and filmed a quick introduction—her thoughts, feelings and a little on the surroundings. Just as she was getting to the end of her piece, she saw a familiar face creeping up behind her on the viewfinder.

'Boo!' Inga wrapped her arms around Eve's waist and smiled for the camera. 'Ready to make the magic happen?'

Eve clicked the button to stop recording and turned to hug Inga properly. 'Hey! Great to see you. Are you excited for today?'

'I am. But I'm nervous too,' Inga admitted. 'I feel like a rebel without Simon. I hope I do him proud.'

'I keep forgetting that your mentor's a guy. I know what you mean, though…it feels weird being left unattended.' Eve had a sudden pang of guilt. She wasn't sure if she'd shared too much or if Sharon would approve of their conversation.

'I think it's to make sure they don't intervene with our vlogs. They can only guide us so far, I suppose.'

'Ah, there you are.' Kate reappeared behind them. 'Mark's just arrived, so are you ready to dye some yarn?' It was obvious from her grin that she loved her job.

Much to Eve's surprise, yarn dyeing wasn't that difficult. In fact, she found the whole process therapeutic. She started off with what she could only describe as sheep-coloured hanks of yarn. These were then tied together, and the dye applied, which were small tablets of colour and vinegar. You could add the colours in any way you saw fit. Eve went for a vibrant tie-dye effect. Then, the yarn was left to soak so that the colour had chance to take.

During their tutorial, Eve paid close attention to the different vlogging techniques the three of them used to depict the same experience. Inga had placed her camera directly in front of her; it only captured her hands as she followed the process. Mark kept stopping and starting his filming to ensure he filmed the session from every angle. Eve had opted for a video diary approach. She filmed the process but talked about what she was doing and why, and how it felt.

As the wool soaked, they had some time to spare. Kate made them all a hot drink and they sat in her cosy living room.

One of the many perks about working from home.

'So, Kate, why 'Lofties'?' Eve tried her hardest not to laugh as Mark suddenly became a wannabe journalist. 'How did you come up with the name?'

'It's all down to my main man, Lofty.' Kate pointed to a framed picture on the mantelpiece of a particularly dashing alpaca in a bow tie. 'He was the start of it all, so I named my business after him.'

'Aw,' Inga cooed, taking a closer look at the photograph.

'He's a handsome chap,' Eve agreed, peeking over Inga's shoulder.

'Was he the beginning of the family business or just your dyeing company?' Mark pressed. He raised his little finger as he brought his cup of tea to his mouth.

Eve noticed Kate bristle a little. 'We've been spinning yarn for years as a family. The farm dates way back to my ancestors. The indie dyeing and Lofty, that's all down to me.'

'Interesting...' Mark said in a bored tone. He scribbled something in his notebook as Kate looked on, her nose wrinkled with disgruntlement.

'Kate, it's a lovely day outside,' Eve tried to quash the sudden atmosphere, 'would you mind if I filmed some exterior shots? Maybe some footage of your beautiful animals?'

'Absolutely.' Kate's grin was back. 'You carry on.'

'I'll come with you.' Inga scrambled to her

feet. 'Promise I won't copy or anything,' she added quickly as they headed outside.

'That Mark's a bit of a jerk,' said Eve when they were well out of earshot.

Inga nodded. 'Indie said he's been like that since day one. But the judges really like him. They think a man winning this competition would do wonders for their reputation.'

Eve raised an eyebrow. 'Surely, they wouldn't have him win this competition purely because of his gender? Doesn't talent have anything to do with it?'

Inga chuckled. 'They awarded you the first round, remember? I wouldn't get too worried.'

Eve felt herself blush. 'Sorry, you're right. I'm just being paranoid.' She tried to laugh it off, but something about their conversation niggled her.

They trekked to some of the farthest pens where they were greeted by two alpacas: one was beige and lethargic whilst the other was ginger and hyperactive. After petting them for a while, which Eve was confident would make a fabulous montage, they moved round the corner to a flock of Kate's sheep. They looked like a mix of black and white clouds milling about on the large expanse of land as they chewed the grass and bleated away happily.

'Oh, I have to get some panoramic shots of

this!' Eve clapped her hands.

'Give me your camera,' Inga stretched out her hand, 'and go stand over there.' She pointed to a spot in the middle of the flock. 'I'll get you the perfect shot.'

Gingerly, Eve handed over her camera, too excited to say no. 'Isn't this cheating?'

'Just get over there,' Inga laughed. She opened Eve's camera and took a few scenic shots. After a few minutes, she suggested that they should head back.

Eve nodded. 'Let's hope Kate hasn't killed Mark.'

Back at the cottage, they found the duo looking over the yarns.

'Perfect timing,' Kate looked up, beaming. 'Do you want to get your cameras out and see what you've all created?'

Kate retrieved Mark's first. It was beautiful—a deep mix of purples and blues, which gave it a gothic edge. 'Gorgeous,' she affirmed.

Eve's tie-dye did not disappoint. It elicited a few oohs and aahs. 'Well done, Eve, that's stunning.' Kate held it up to make sure the camera caught the explosion of colours.

Kate pulled up Inga's yarn. It looked completely different to the first two—it was a murky charcoal grey. 'Something must have infiltrated the dye. I'm so sorry, Inga.'

Inga's camera was rolling. Despite her best efforts to act casual about the whole thing, Eve could see tears welling in her eyes. 'That's okay,' she said to Kate, her voice faltering slightly. 'I'll still be able to create something awesome with it.'

'That's the spirit,' said Kate. 'You never really know what you're going to get with yarn dyeing.'

Eve caught Inga's gaze as they left shortly after. Her eyes were dull; her usual sparkle had diminished. In fact, her face was a similar shade of grey as her disastrously dyed yarn. There was a sense of foreboding in the air, Eve could feel it in her stomach.

Chapter Eleven

Once at her dad's, Eve wasted no time uploading her videos to her laptop and watching them back. She was happy to find that all of her footage was usable. Her favourite element was the panoramic shot Inga had taken of her in the sheep pen.

'That's definitely my opening,' Eve muttered to herself. Thinking of Inga, she visited her Facebook page. She hadn't been online since early that morning. Eve sent her a message asking how she was.

Sometimes, it's just nice to know someone's there.

***

A couple of days later, Inga had turned her disaster into a learning curve. She sent a reply to Eve's message: *People will just think I'm human. I've shown a realistic portrayal of a 'first go'. I think I've got this.*

In the meantime, Eve had downloaded all the (free) video editing software available and tried them with little success. On day three, after admitting defeat, she asked Inga for help. She didn't see the harm.

Hi, Inga! How's your editing going? I have absolutely no idea what I'm doing!

Inga's response was immediate.

Oh my god, me neither! Currently trying to get hold of my brother. He's the best computer geek I know! I'll let you know if he has any advice. X

Eve sighed—she'd hoped Inga had a miracle up her sleeve. Then she realised the answer was there. She knew a computer geek too, the best in town. *But will she answer my call?*

On the third attempt, Jemma picked up.

'Thank god,' Eve sighed. 'For a moment there, I didn't think you were going to pick up.'

There was an awkward pause on the other end of line. 'That's because I wasn't.'

'Oh…' Eve didn't know what to say.

'Eve, it's not the same without you around,' Jemma gushed. 'Since you left, Sim refuses to talk about it. The only thing she'll say is that you let fame go to your head. Honestly, she's acting like you don't exist—it's vile! She'd kill me if she knew I'd answered your call.'

'Oh,' Eve said again, searching for the right words. 'I'd no idea that Sim has taken this so badly. She hasn't responded to my messages or calls, but I thought she was just in one of her moods…'

'She feels like you've run out on her in her time of need. After the whole thing with Jack and everything…'

Eve felt a lump in her throat. 'But I thought everything was okay? You said that at

Browndales...that she'd come round.'

'I thought she would. But I was wrong.' There was another silence. 'Why did you call?'

'I need your help,' Eve admitted, though her editing nightmare seemed insignificant now. 'It was in relation to video editing, but maybe now, it's about fixing my mistakes.'

'Have you got work tomorrow?'

'Yes. I'm on earlies. 9am-2pm.'

'I'll meet you after your shift,' said Jem. 'Bring your laptop.'

***

The next day, at 1.55pm, Jemma strode into The Bean & Mug. She threw her bag and jacket down on the cosy seats and approached the counter.

'Hey,' Eve smiled.

'Hey,' Jemma smiled in return.

Butterflies fluttered in Eve's stomach; she felt slightly giddy at seeing her friend again. She couldn't believe it had been so long. 'You can be my last customer of the day. What can I get you?'

'Erm, I'll have a hot chocolate, please, and whatever you're having.' Jemma rummaged around in her pockets for change.

'I'll get one at the next place,' Eve said as she pushed the buttons on the till.

'You'll be thirsty then, as I was planning to

stay here until we were done.'

'Here?!' Eve hadn't intended to say that as loud as it came out—Tony was only metres behind her at the barista station. He was, however, facing a losing battle with the milk frother.

'It's the safest place,' said Jemma as she handed Eve a ten-pound note. 'Sim wouldn't dream of stepping foot in here at the moment. I'll get set up.'

Hanging up her apron, Eve grabbed her bag and laptop from the staffroom and took them to the table Sim had claimed. She then collected their drinks and carried them over.

'It's a good job I love you,' Eve hissed as she placed the two mugs down. 'This place already consumes way too much of my time.'

Eve booted up her laptop and watched in fascination as Jem scoured the web for software. 'Here,' Jem handed her back the laptop, 'I'm going to try you with this. I haven't really used it much since I was at uni, but it has a very user-friendly interface. We should be fine.'

Eve looked at Jem innocently.

'What?' she laughed. 'I'm teaching you how to do it, I'm not doing it for you. So, you'll be able to do your own in the future. I can't hold your hand forever. Aren't you glad I got you that coffee now?'

Jemma dodged as one of the cosy cushions, aptly shaped like a coffee bean, was launched at her head.

Just under four hours later, Eve clicked to add the final finishing touches to her vlog. Jemma was curled up in the corner in a hot chocolate coma after drinking four cups. Eve's second cappuccino sat behind her laptop screen, stone cold.

'Finished!' she squeaked, making Jemma jump out of her skin.

'W-huh?' Jem looked over, bleary-eyed.

'I think I'm done! Want to have a look?'

'Sure.' Jem straightened in her seat. As she did so, her girlfriend, Rosie, came into the coffee shop looking flustered. 'Hey, babe! Everything okay?' Jem jumped up to give her a kiss.

'I've been looking all over for you. Does Sim know you're here?' Rosie gave Eve a sideways glance.

'Hi,' Eve attempted, but Rosie wasn't interested.

'Nope.'

'That's probably for the best. No offence, Eve, it's just things haven't been great since you left.'

She nodded glumly and turned back to her

computer screen to avoid the awkwardness.

'We'd best go, Jem,' Rosie cooed. 'There's just enough time to get you fed and watered before bedtime. You promised you'd get an early night, remember? Big day tomorrow!'

'Oh?' Eve looked over the top of her laptop.

'Yeah.' Jem looked uncomfortable all of a sudden. 'I managed to get an internship with the Berlington Gazette. It's my first day tomorrow. This one thinks I've landed chief editor at The Guardian.'

'Shoot me for being proud of my girlfriend!' Rosie weaved her arm through Jemma's in a bid to get her to leave.

'Bye!' Jemma managed to call over shoulder. 'Good luck with your vlog.'

'Thanks!' Eve called back. 'Good luck with the internship!' she added awkwardly.

As she collected her things, she couldn't help feeling guilty. She reminded herself that she wasn't the one acting stubborn and childish. All the same, in her absence, things were moving forward without her. Her friends were doing the same as she was…progressing, living, doing what they should be doing. *Good for them.* But she wasn't there to support them like she knew she should be, and that part hurt more than she cared to admit.

23rd April 2019

Amazing Opportunities

Hey, guys,
I'm in the thick of the Indigo Blue Superstar Search—I can't believe I'm about to hand in task two!

I'm making some lovely new friendships, but I'm also missing others. Have you ever felt that, in order to better yourself, you've had to miss out on some important events with your loved ones? Let me know if you understand where I'm coming from, as any advice would be amazing right now. If I'm being brutally honest, I'm feeling like a crap friend at the minute.

Okay, okay, let's move on. I'm having a fantastic time in this competition. Honestly, I'm so glad I was given this amazing opportunity.

I don't want to write too much because I don't want to give anything away that I'm not meant to. Remember, you can view my progress and vote for me during the different tasks over on Indigo's social media pages.

In the meantime, I hope you're all doing well. Let me know what I'm missing in the crochet world in the comments. I'm out of the loop on so many things, because I'm just so busy!

Hooks and Kisses
Eve xx

Views: 12,878
Comments: 504
HookedOnCrochet: Hang in there, girl. You're doing amazing!

Chapter Twelve

The week in which the videos went live passed by in a blur.

Eve was preoccupied with her feelings of guilt and sadness to really care about her view counter. However, she did watch all three vlogs and felt happy with her effort.

In the downtime, she decided to take a break. She'd tried messaging and texting Sim on various occasions and still received no response. Even contact with Jem was thin on the ground now she was working more sociable hours. Eve turned back to her first love to fill the void. Her dad's hat complete and now warming his head, it was time for her to start a new project.

She'd made a makeshift wool den from a bookcase in her office; Eve looked over the small selection of balls that had made the cut. Because the move to her dad's was temporary, she'd not brought her whole collection with her. It was wool from Indigo's various collections that Eve was yet to use, and given the whole point of the competition, she knew she needed to. She ran her fingers across the different textures. Some were smooth and silky whilst others were thick and coarse. Some had little bobbles in their make-up, whilst others felt like fluffy eyelashes. Her hand paused on a particularly chunky-but-super-snuggly yarn in hot pink. It was from one of Indigo's first collections: Go Big or Go Home. Each one of those yarns has been super chunky, in a colour palette designed to catch the eye; this one was no exception. She had purchased it on the day the collection was launched, partly persuaded by Sim who had been looking over her shoulder at the time. Eve pulled six huge balls down from the shelf. She knew exactly what she was going to do.

In her dad's living room, with some of her crocheted blankets draped around her for comfort and motivation, Eve trawled the web for a pattern. She knew what she was after—something chic but functional. Something that would turn heads, but which you could wear every day. Something bright and happy. Something very *Simone*. Eve looked at pattern after pattern…from gloves to hats to jumpers and dresses. Nothing seemed quite right. Then she found it.

The idea was simple enough. The cardigan was made in one piece from cuff to cuff; it increased for the main body and decreased back down again. It was designed to cocoon the wearer. Aptly named a snug, Eve felt it was perfect for the yarn she'd chosen. The design was predominantly made with a 15mm hook, which was exactly what her yarn recommended. It couldn't be more perfect. Eve entered her card details and downloaded her new pattern. A fuzzy feeling bubbled up inside her. *This was going to be the olive branch.* A funny looking, luminous-pink olive branch, but an olive branch all the same. Peacefully, she hooked on her foundation chain with ease. She knew that everything was going to work out fine.

From that point, Eve crocheted everywhere. At home, in public, during journeys to the grocery shop in her dad's car, standing up on the train—you name it. She'd even attempted to crochet whilst walking, but that didn't go down so well. It turns out that you need to look where you're going.

The cardigan came along at a fantastic pace. It was more than enough to keep Eve's motivation and energy flowing. She was already into the increases, and the perfection on her front and back post trebles made the cuff and border look divine.

Soon, the next Superstar Search meeting rolled around. 'The problem is, these balls are really bulky. They're awkward to carry around.' She was due at Indigo Blue HQ the following day and Eve hoped her dad would steer her one way or the other as to whether she should/shouldn't take her crochet.

He picked up one of the balls. 'Geez, these are big!' he said with wide eyes, before putting it back down swiftly. 'But you'll want to crochet on the train.'

'True. But it's not just that. I'd be taking my crochet into the world inhabited by crochet royalty. I'll be judged on my skill, my colour choice...my tension!'

Her dad looked at her philosophically. 'Aren't they judging your crochet anyway?'

'This is different. This is my *personal* crochet.'

'Maybe keep it in your bag?' he suggested.

'Daaad! Eve sighed dramatically. 'These people are like crochet sniffer dogs. It'll get ratted out somehow, I just know it. And I think that's worse...' She trailed off as she pictured how such a discovery would unfold in a group meeting. Would it be seen as an advantage? One-upmanship? A secret side task? Would she be disqualified? Eve's mind was used to overthinking, but now it ran away with her.

'Do it with pride then. Like a badge of honour. Walk in, crocheting, unfazed.'

She raised an eyebrow. 'Oh, I don't know-'

'It's all about confidence.' her dad persisted. 'You love your craft so much you'll do it *anywhere!*'

'Actually...that's a good idea.' Her dad smiled. 'Yeah! Everyone will feel the need to up their game after that.' She was almost sold on the idea. 'Are you sure I won't look like a show off?'

Her dad shook his head confidently. 'No! I think you'll look fantastic.' He began stuffing one of the oversized pink balls into her commuting bag.

***

The next day, with her crochet packed, she headed for the train. Once on board, she spared no time getting out her hook, cardigan, and wool, and getting to work. She knew that, if she could get into the rhythm of it, she'd make it look easy by the time she walked into Blue HQ.

Yarn over, insert hook. Yarn over, pull through stitch. Yarn over, pull through all loops on hook. Repeat.

She was instantly absorbed. In fact, she got so into it that she paid no attention to the suave-looking businessman in the tweed suit who took the vacant seat beside her. She didn't seem to notice how much her elbow jutted out with the rhythm of her stitches, like she was playing a violin, even though she was invading his personal space.

It wasn't until the train conductor announced

the next stop that she noticed him at all. As she scooped up her crochet and stuffed it into her tote bag, she found it a bit peculiar that he returned her pleasant smile with a scowl. In fact, Eve thought him so rude that she almost didn't apologise as the thrust of the train practically jolted her into the poor man's lap when she got up to leave. What had she done wrong? As she made her way out of the station, she couldn't help but feel it was a sign. If her live crochet skills hadn't impressed the guy on the train, what would the real critics think?

***

She was one of the first to arrive at Blue HQ. From the moment she stepped inside, she sensed an atmosphere. Everyone she greeted was either curt in response or they failed to hold eye contact. She'd felt from the off that Indigo's team hadn't been the friendliest of people; they were much colder and more corporate than she would have ever imagined—but she thought she'd got past basic pleasantries.

As she entered the conference room, she saw a group of the higher-ups huddled in the corner, whispering. Seeing Eve, they fell silent, and from the centre of the huddle, Sharon's slightly flushed face popped up. 'Eve! Great to see you. We're just finishing up here. Would you mind waiting outside for a second? I'll come and get you when we're ready.'

'Okay.' She retreated, feeling awkward. In the corridor, her mind began to reel with thoughts of what they'd been talking about. The next task? The finalists' progress? The public vote? Who they thought should win? Who they thought should *lose*?

Her hands were clammy. She needed a distraction and remembered the crochet in her bag. She whipped it out and started hooking away, her worries dissipating with every stitch. As she relaxed into her rhythm, she was completely immersed. She could have been crocheting for two minutes or two days. By the time Sharon came to collect her, she'd almost forgotten about the secret huddle.

'You can come in now.' Sharon paused as she spotted what Eve was doing. 'This is beautiful.' She delicately ran her hand along the piece. 'What's it going to be?'

'A cardigan.' Eve felt she'd made the right decision, bringing her crochet along.

'For yourself?' Sharon couldn't take her eyes off it.

'For a friend.' Eve stopped to look at her crochet too. She really hoped Sim would like it. More to the point, she hoped she'd accept it.

'Well, please come in. Andrew wants to get

things started as quickly as possible. There's something important you all need to know before we proceed.'

The sweaty palms and pang in her stomach returned as she followed Sharon. Mark and Hayley filed in behind her with Inga and Simon bringing up the rear. Instead of sitting down, Inga and Simon stood at Andrew's side. Inga's head was bowed.

'Good afternoon, glad to have you all here.' Andrew cleared his throat and fidgeted with his tie. 'Before I continue with our normal proceedings, Inga has an announcement.' He stepped back and gestured for her to take the floor. There were easily twenty people in the room, but you could have heard a pin drop (and there were plenty of pins around).

'Hello, everyone.' Inga's voice broke on her first word. 'I'm not going to drag this out. Over the last week Simon and I have had some serious conversations. I wanted to address you all, rather than slip away in the dead of night. In light of the error made in my vlog experience, and together with my anxieties and other personal issues, we've mutually agreed that the Superstar search is no longer for me, so I'm stepping back from the competition. I just wanted to thank you all for this amazing opportunity...' She trailed off and Eve saw her bottom lip quiver. Indigo got up and pulled her into a tight hug. Inga's shoulders lifted and fell as she sobbed.

Andrew stepped forward and coughed awkwardly. 'If anyone would like to say their goodbyes, now would be the time to do so.'

Mark stepped forward—reluctantly, Eve noted—and shook Inga's hand. He said a few words to her then stepped away again. Inga turned to Eve; her damp eyes were bloodshot.

'I'm going to miss you,' said Eve.

'I'll miss you too. But it's for the best.' As they hugged, Inga whispered in her ear, 'It got out that Indigo and I had an online friendship, pre-competition. Be careful, Eve. They'll be on the lookout for anything to use as a distraction to cover this up. You've got to win this—for me, you, and Indigo. You deserve to.' When they pulled away, Eve nodded in agreement.

Goodbyes over, Indigo glared at Andrew Benson before helping Inga with her suitcase. She gave one last wave before she left.

The room fell silent. It was so awkward that Eve seriously contemplated getting out her crochet again. On reflection, she didn't want to attract any attention.

'And then there were two.' There was a wicked grin on Andrew's lips that made her feel rather nauseated. 'So...onto the next task.' He rubbed his hands together and picked up his notes.

'We would like you to do a week-long takeover of Indigo's social media platforms. Your week's content must include at least three live videos—the subject of which will be down to you; a never-ending story feed that can be archived into a highlight at the end of the week; and six feed posts...and we would love it if you could get at least one of your unique hashtags trending. You'll get one full week's takeover, Monday to Sunday, on Indigo's multiple platforms. Again, we shall review all of your content and nominate a winner, but we shall also go to the public vote at the end of the week. You have one week's prep time from now and Indigo will demonstrate to you both what your week might look like. I wish you both the best of luck. See you on the other side.'

He nodded to a few people before leaving the room. Emily scurried after him.

Eve turned to Sharon. 'Will Indigo ever announce any of her tasks?'

Sharon did her best to stifle a laugh. 'Pfft! Pigs might fly. Come on.'

In their pod, Sharon was on it straightaway. 'Realistically, how much time can you dedicate to the week? Any chance of a holiday from work...or even a sick week?' She eyed Eve in earnest.

'If I was creating a week's worth of live content for social media, I'm pretty sure my boss would see I wasn't sick. I could lose my job.' Sharon didn't even flinch. 'I'll ask about a holiday,' she sighed.

'Fabulous. Now, I've arranged for you to watch one of Indigo's videos being filmed. I thought it might be beneficial for you to see firsthand the standard expected. How does next Friday suit you?'

'Fine, actually, it's my day off.' Eve gave a smile of relief.

'I'm actually busy that day,' Sharon continued. 'I have an appointment with some of our wool suppliers, which, unfortunately, I can't change. You'll be okay taking yourself, right? I'll give you the postcode and I'll make sure everyone's aware of the situation.'

Finally! It was what she'd been waiting for—a behind the scenes insight into the life of Indigo Blue.

'Yes, that's fine by me. Thank you, Sharon.'

She brushed away Eve's words. 'Don't thank me yet.' She reached into her bag to retrieve her notebook and pen. 'Right, let's get down to business.'

***

Three days later, Eve was working her shift at

The Bean & Mug, daydreaming as she served customers. Her week's worth of content was bothering her. Together with Sharon, she'd come up with a skeleton of an idea about what she should do; however, the 'meat' was still very much down to her.

Today, Eve was on barista duty—latte art being her personal expertise. But no matter how many hearts she swirled into the milk, creativity in any other form just wasn't flowing.

'A caramel double-choca-mocha and a large tea to drink in,' Emma's monotone voice rang out.

The drink order sparked some excitement within her. Looking up, she saw the back of 'Caramel Double-Choca-Mocha' walking to his table, his excessively long scarf trailing behind him.

Eve concocted the quickest caramel double-choca-mocha she'd ever made. She thrust her pinny in Emma's direction, much to her annoyance, and carried the drinks to Caramel Double-Choca-Mocha's table. She glanced back at Emma, who was tying the apron round her waist and cleaning the steamer. *Perfect. This was her chance. All her woollen prayers had been answered.*

'Hey, Caramel Double-Choca-Mocha guy!' Eve said in her chirpiest voice.

'Er, hi?' The guy looked taken aback by his nickname. Eve thought he had a lovely, kind face. His eyes twinkled under a mop of black hair and his thick-rimmed glasses. A small smile appeared; he looked rather bemused at the forthrightness of the barista before him. He shared his table with a fiery redhead. Her hair was gorgeous...corkscrew curls cascaded around her shoulders and down her back. She smiled at Eve. She wore the most elegant, knitted waterfall cardigan Eve had ever seen. The craftsmanship was *insane.* Eve made a mental note: *do not become distracted by the amazing woollen wizardry.*

Eve held up the two mugs she carried.

'Ah, thank you,' the guy said, running his hand through his hair (something Eve had seen him do a lot—it was like a habit).

'One caramel double-choca-mocha,' she placed this down in front of the gent, 'and a large cup of tea.' She put this in front of the redhead.

Eve didn't want to appear a stalker, but she recognised the guy from elsewhere. 'You're the owner of the wool shop in Rosworth, right?' She squirmed a little as she watched the couple swap drinks.

'Yes! Anything I can help you with?'

Bingo.

'Actually, I have a massive favour to ask. I've been asked to create some online content for this competition I'm a part of. I'm not sure if you've heard of the crochet influencer- '

The guy nodded at the redhead. 'You're better off talking to this one about all that new age technical stuff.' He chuckled then took a swig of his tea.

'I'm Claire,' the redhead said, smiling. 'I'm the caramel double-choca-mocha addict. Adrian here prefers the simpler pleasures in life.' She winked at him.

'I'm sorry,' Eve blushed at her own presumptuousness as she took Claire's outstretched hand. 'I'm Eve.'

'I knew it!' Claire said excitedly. 'You're one of Indigo Blue's Superstars, aren't you?'

'Yes!' Eve felt her blush deepen. 'You recognise me?'

'Yeah,' she nodded. 'I'm loving the competition. To be honest, I'm *hooked*!' The two women laughed at the pun.

'Claire's recently been introduced to the world of crochet.' Adrian interjected, resting his mug on the table. 'Please excuse her enthusiasm—she's become a little addicted to her laptop. I'm pretty sure, at this point, she's watched every crochet video in existence.'

'Shut up, you.' She tapped his hand

playfully.

#couplegoals

'We'd love to help you. Us local wool lovers have got to stick together,' said Claire.

'Sure,' Adrian nodded. 'And any promotion of our business would be greatly received.'

'Perfect!' Eve tried not to get too excited; the last thing she wanted to do was attract Tony's attention from across the café, but this couple's energy was just infectious. 'Would it be okay if I swung by next week and filmed a little interview with you about some of the current hot topics in the woolly world?'

Adrian nodded, and Claire practically bounced in her seat. 'I can do better than that! Why don't you pop by next Wednesday and talk to our 'Knit and Knatter' group? I'm sure they'll have plenty to say. I promise they'll give you some fantastic content.'

'You can say that again,' Adrian smiled.

'EVE!' She jumped as her name was bellowed across the café. Emma looked more than a little mad.

'I've got to go.' She smiled awkwardly. 'But that sounds perfect! See you then. Thanks again—you've been such a great help.'

'Come by about 2pm,' Claire called as Eve hurried away. 'I'll let the ladies know you're coming.'

Chapter Thirteen

Eve arrived at the address Sharon had given her, ahead of schedule. She'd largely found her way with Google Maps, but in reality, she had no idea where she was. She got out of the taxi she'd taken for the last part of her journey and faced a tall, iron gate with an intercom at its side. After giving her name, she was buzzed in; Simon, Inga's mentor, met her at the door of the large three-storey home.

'Welcome to Le Chateau Blue,' Simon said in a poor French accent.

This is Indigo's home? Eve was dazed. She knew that Indigo had the life of a rock star, but she'd not expected this.

'Come in, come in,' he beckoned. 'We're just setting up.'

Eve followed him through the hall and reception room, which had multiple doors leading off them. They headed up a staircase onto a landing with more doors. They turned past those and went up another flight of stairs to a spacious loft conversion. As they emerged from the stairwell into the room itself, Eve drew a sharp breath. It was Indigo's bedroom, and it was exactly how it looked in her videos. The crochet wall hanging that had taken her over a year to craft; and the king-sized bed on which she sat to chat about her favourite products, with its ever-changing granny square cushions and elaborate throws. A mannequin tucked in the corner showcasing her latest completed project—it was all there. Right now, though, it resembled a film set.

Indigo was in position, perched on the end of her bed. She was studying a notebook intently, muttering what Eve presumed were her lines.

A girl with a belt-bag full of brushes was applying make-up to her face. A camera was on a tripod in the centre of the room. Zipping around it was another girl with short, spiky blonde hair; she set up rings of light and moved them around to get the best angles. A guy wrestled with a fluffy boom mic.

Behind the camera, Emily barked orders at the various people around her. This was not the vlogging environment Eve had expected. It felt...clinical. The cosy, homely vibe that Eve normally got from Indigo's videos was destroyed, now that she'd seen it from the other side of the camera.

'Ready and...ACTION!' Emily suddenly snapped. Everything in front of the camera, bar Indigo, cleared away. She looked small and alone under the spotlight. But she sprang into action on cue, and soon lit up the room with her trademark smile and bouncy blue curls.

In today's video she was reviewing a set of light-up crochet hooks.

'STOP!' Emily barked at Indigo mid-sentence. 'We need more Indigo. More passion. More excitement!'

'Set!' On Emily's word, two girls rushed over to reset Indigo's hair and make-up.

'And ACTION!' Indigo went again...and again and again.

'CUT!' Emily called for the fifth time. 'What's wrong, Indigo? You're flinching every time you move the hook.'

'It's just...when I crochet with them...they squeak. It's the kind of plastic they've used. It puts my teeth on edge, like fingernails down a chalkboard.'

'Can someone oil the crochet hook, please?' Emily's drawl said it all. 'This company is paying us a lot of money. We need to make their product look desirable.'

Instantly, a woman appeared with what looked like a tin of lip balm. She took the hook, slathered it with the balm then handed it back, much to Indigo's distaste.

Imagine crocheting with a greasy hook. The thought made Eve shudder a little.

'Right then, places! ACTION!'

Eve watched awkwardly from the back of the room as the scene played out again and again.

She saw Indigo becoming increasingly uncomfortable as the takes went on. When the camera went live, she put on her trademark smile in a flash, but Eve could tell she was faking her energy.

'The price of fame, eh?' Simon reappeared and spoke softly in Eve's ear. 'What do you think of this set up? Not what you expected, I presume?' She nodded, a little overwhelmed by it all to make a comment. Simon continued, 'You see, that's the thing these days, it's all about your online persona. Not the reality anymore. We need to make it look as cosy and as homely as possible for Indigo's viewers. Because cosy and homely is what they want; it's the vibe Indigo has projected all these years. It's just that, now, we have to produce it in high definition. It's why Sharon wanted you here today. The competition's heating up. You need to pin down your vibe. Be 100% concrete on what you want your image to be.'

Eve didn't know what she wanted her image to be. Watching everything unfolding in front of her, the only word that came to mind was 'authentic'—something that this video clearly couldn't mimic. Before she could express this to Simon, she heard a low buzzing sound.

Simon retrieved his phone from his pocket. 'I need to take this,' he whispered. 'But stay as long as you like, be inspired. We'll talk soon.' He left her to her thoughts.

'THAT'S A WRAP!' called Emily. Eve noticed that everyone around her visibly relaxed.

Filming complete, she watched the team dismantle everything and pack it all away into flight cases.

'Eve! How lovely to see you. Have you come to see how the magic happens?' Indigo said when she was free to talk. Eve noticed little beads of sweat had formed on her bright blue hairline.

'Absolutely,' Eve smiled. 'Want to grab a drink or something? That looked stressful.'

'I'd love to.' She bit her lip. 'Do you think that's wise?' She shifted her eyes towards the many team members that were still milling about. Again, the almost tangible yet unspoken rule that Indigo shouldn't spend time alone with the contestants reared its head. And with Inga's early departure still fresh in people's minds, there was a noticeable coolness in the atmosphere. Today, under all the spotlights and layers of hair and make-up, Eve had seen a vulnerability to Indigo that she couldn't ignore. She needed someone to talk to, and Eve was a good listener. 'I'd just like to ask you a few things about the process, in preparation for my content next week. I promise it won't take long.'

Indigo nodded. 'Just hover for a little while. I won't be long.'

The crew began to leave. Bit by bit, the film set disappeared until the room resembled the bedroom Eve was used to seeing. She managed to remain unnoticed by helping to carry various objects to their storage spots. It was the perfect disguise, hiding in plain sight.

'Right, I believe we're done here.' Emily was the last to leave. 'I'll have someone look through your PO box again tomorrow and I'll send you anything that may be of interest. Speak soon.' Without waiting for Indigo's reply, she turned on her heel and was gone.

Indigo flopped down on her bed. 'That's the last of them,' she called to Eve, who stepped out of her makeshift hiding place in the corner of the room. 'How about that coffee?'

Indigo led her down to the first floor of the house. She opened a door into a beautiful kitchen, which contained every mod-con you could want. Indigo grabbed two mugs from the rack and flicked a switch on the coffee machine. 'Take a seat.' She gestured towards her marble breakfast bar. Eve hopped up obligingly on one of the stools, her mind whirring over how much a kitchen like Indigo's must have cost.

'Wow!' It slipped out as her eyes scanned the

room.

Indigo smiled as she placed the two mugs on the counter. 'I'm kind of gutted. I've lost that feeling when I look at this place.' She was still smiling but there was a sadness in her eyes.

'What do you mean?' Eve wrapped her hands around the warm mug gratefully. 'You're living the dream here. What's not to love?'

'That's exactly it. Everything's become a dream now. It's all make-believe. I mean, take today for example, I don't just talk to my camera as a hobby anymore…or for escapism. It's a military operation!'

'I could tell you felt uncomfortable,' Eve admitted. 'I did think it was all a little…'extra', but if it gets the job done…' She trailed off after seeing the look on Indigo's face.

'Nothing is *real* anymore! Everything's been changed, distorted…the truth about everything has been stretched in one way or another.' Her voice dropped. 'This isn't even my real hair colour, you know.'

Eve had to deploy restraint to every muscle in her body to stop herself from laughing. She wasn't sure if Indigo had been joking. 'If that's how you feel, why are you still here, performing to their every will? I'm so sorry to have to say this, and I don't want to offend you, but you've become their puppet.' She said that last sentence without really thinking, but what she'd seen had really struck a chord with her.

Indigo let out an almighty sob. 'I know! I know I am!'

Eve hopped down from the breakfast bar to wrap a supportive arm around her shoulders. The floodgates had been opened, and Eve could feel her distress.

'At first, it was the money.' Indigo pulled a rainbow granny square from her pocket to blow her nose. 'I was living my dream life! I could have anything I wanted. Anything at all. All I had to do was go along with what they said. At first, I didn't mind, because it didn't stray far from what I was already doing: dyeing yarn, testing patterns, reviewing crochet hooks. Overnight, my opinion didn't matter. I reviewed absolutely anything that related to wool: sock blockers, row counters, even buttons! It got to the stage where there was so much stuff, I didn't even have the time to figure out how to use half of it. I mean, does anyone know how to use a Saxony spinning wheel on their first attempt?'

'I've never even heard of a Saxony spinning wheel!' Eve laughed, which made her smile.

'Exactly! It was such a stress. I started being told by my team whether or not something was good. And with all the pressure, I just trusted that what we were saying was right.' She reached for her granny square hankie again. 'Then the letters started coming. Brands complaining about my reviews. Legal threats. Death threats! You name it, I've seen it. Honestly, people feel anonymous online; they don't care what they say from the safety of their screen. I had to develop a thick skin, quickly. I thought my team was protecting me. If I'd left them then, I'd have been out there on my own with those scary people.'

'Gosh, Indigo, why didn't you speak out about this online? I'm sure we could have helped you. At the root of it, you have a loving, loyal community that could have seen you through it all.'

'I thought about that,' she said, 'but Andrew said it could ruin my career. I just had to stick with it. It was the fear of it all.'

'That's horrible.' Eve shook her head. 'Your lifestyle always looked so glamorous from the outside.'

'Wait, there's more!' Indigo raised a finger before blowing her nose like a trumpet. 'Next, it was the designs. They wanted me to start designing my own patterns using my yarn. But I hadn't the foggiest idea what to do. I've been following patterns my whole life! They sent me on this course, but I just couldn't grasp it. So, they employed ghost designers. You'll be meeting them soon for the task.' Eve's eyes widened. *Ghost designers? How had the company managed to keep that secret? That little snippet of information would have been worth a lot of money in the wrong hands.*

'My life has become a lie,' Indigo said ruefully, unable to stop now she'd started. 'One big, fat lie. But it's so far along now, with so many webs interweaving, I don't know what I can do to stop it.'

She slumped in her seat—and suddenly looked so...ordinary. Like any other woman Eve's age who had the weight of the world on her shoulders. The blue hair, the crazy crocheted clothes, the big personality...they didn't seem to matter. She was a frightened, distressed twenty-something who didn't know what to do with her life. Eve could certainly relate to that. They were on exactly the same page.

'Come on,' said Eve. 'I'm going to help you solve this.'

The two women spent the rest of the afternoon with their heads together, concocting a plan. They lost all track of time and Eve had to race to the iron gates to greet her taxi. Indigo waved from the doorway.

Neither woman noticed someone watching

them from across the street.

***

Back at her dad's, Eve lay back on the bed and thought about the situation more and more. Anger rose inside her. This glamorous online life, this crochet paradise she'd been watching from the sidelines for so long— pouring money into, pining after—it was all a hideous lie. How could those people live with themselves, knowing that they were ruining a bright, young girl with a creative flair and a golden heart? Indigo's only fault had been her naivety. It was money, fame and greed that had built the monsters.

She sighed and pulled the duvet high over her head. It was ugly, wrong, and, truth be told, a sad situation that had become bigger and more pressing than any competition. Something had to be done, and it looked like Eve was going to be the one to do it.

Chapter Fourteen

'And if we could refrain from secret midnight chats with Indigo.' Andrew looked Eve dead in the eye. With just one day to go before the online takeover, Eve received a last-minute email offering her a 'once in a lifetime opportunity' to have a one-on-one meeting with Andrew Benson. Right now, Eve felt the email had just been an elaborate rouse to pass on a warning.

'Were you trying to better your chances, perhaps? It won't work...you're just wasting your time. The overall decisions are always made by me.' He gave a weird grin.

Eve hadn't been in the meeting long; she'd been running late and had to race up to Andrew's office as a result. That the conversation had been so dark as soon as she'd sat down was a bit of a shock. She didn't know how to react to his words.

He briskly changed the subject. 'Back to business. I hear from Sharon that you have your week's content planned and ready to go.'

She nodded. It was mostly there, but time seemed to have run away with her a little. She'd have to crowbar into her diary the time to fine-tune what she had planned or, worst case scenario, she'd just have to leave it to fate and go with what she'd got.

'Fantastic. I've got you here today to go through some basic rules for when you're in control of one of our biggest assets.' There was that weird grin again. She felt the anger begin to bubble again. *They really do see Indigo as just a cash cow, don't they?*

He continued, outlining the dos and don'ts of her week, e.g. no swearing; remembering to sign out after every session and sign back in when she returned; specific hashtags she had to use; ensuring third parties were tagged appropriately, etc. Eve listened, but inside her head she picked him apart. She inwardly recoiled when he wagged his stumpy fingers around, like he was reprimanding a child, and she found it amusing that his shirt buttons were clinging on for dear life, poorly disguised by his tie. His hair sported too much gel, which gave it a sticky finish. And whilst the permanent dimples in his cheeks suggested a boyish charm, the deep lines in his furrows told a different story. He was an accurate representation of most managers she had encountered. He was just a guy who'd got lucky...who'd took a chance on a bright, young star at the right time.

'Andrew, can you crochet?' Before Eve could consider the fallout of such a question, it had already left her lips.

'Pardon?'

'Sorry, I was just curious. Being such a main player in this industry, I figure you'd have your finger on the pulse—or the hook, as it were.'

'Well...' he fiddled with his tie, 'I have picked up a crochet hook from time to time. But Indigo's the real talent when it comes to that sort of thing. I just deal with all the ugly, commercial, business stuff. Someone's got to have the brains.' He laughed. A hearty, alpha-male kind of laugh.

'Of course.' Eve smiled sweetly. 'Well, I think I understand everything that's required of me. Is there anything else?'

'Erm, no, I think we've covered it all.'

'Perfect. In that case, I'd better get back. I want to get an early night, in preparation for tomorrow.' She began to gather her things.

'Good idea. Thank you, Eve. I look forward to seeing what you come up with.'

***

Indigo Blue: *Are you ready?*
Eve Jay: *As ready as I'll ever be!*
Indigo Blue: *Here we go...*

***

When Eve refreshed her feed the next morning, a picture of her smiling face stared back at her. This was it.

Instantly, a new message landed in her inbox: *Sharon Harrison: Username – indigoblue; Password - superstarsearch002. Good Luck!*

With quivering fingers, Eve logged out of her social accounts and into Indigo Blue's. She glanced around her makeshift office. Everything was set; there wasn't a hook or ball of wool out of place. It was showtime. She started a live video and held her phone out in front of her. 'Hey, guys! It's Eve here, kicking off my week's content for Indigo Blue as part of her Superstar Search! Right now, I'm talking to you from sunny Berlington in the UK.'

Across the bottom of the screen, Eve saw a flurry of names, comments and love hearts appear. She forced herself to ignore them, fearing it may trigger stage fright. 'The plan is to take you around with me, so you can walk through a week of my life and see just how much crochet is a part of it. I also have surprises in store with some special guests. I promise you, my content is not to be missed, so fasten your seatbelts and hold onto your hooks!'

'You've got this,' she reassured herself as she turned off the live function and started uploading her posts into the different platforms' draft folders.

Day one of her takeover week was a huge

success—her live video got more than a million views by the end of the first day. She interacted with more than a hundred of Indigo's fans via comments and direct messages, and her introductory post racked up more and more likes as the hours went by. She didn't watch any of Mark's content, as she just wanted to focus on her work, but assumed it was performing in a similar manner. When she logged out for the evening, she couldn't help feeling chuffed with how things had gone.

The following day, Eve planned to make the content all about crochet—after all, she figured, that's what Indigo's audience was after. On Indigo's stories and her feed, she walked followers through her personal crochet hall of fame. She showcased her crochet loves and made sure to tag every yarn company and pattern designer mentioned. It was a bit of an effort. Halfway through, Eve regretted starting the topic. She dismissed her negative thoughts; she'd reap the rewards of her hard work when big brands in the wool world shared her posts.

Day three rolled around, which was the day Eve had been waiting for. It was the day of her appointment at Adrian and Claire's wool shop, 'Oddballs'.

Before the takeover week began, Eve had researched this quaint local business. The more she learned about Oddballs, the guiltier she felt. Eve Jay—an avid wool user who hadn't ever stepped foot inside her local wool shop. Today, she was going to right that wrong.

***

'Perfect timing!' Claire jumped up from her seat; she'd been practically buried in yarn. She greeted her with a warm hug. 'Come on in, we've got just enough time to set you up before the ladies arrive.'

'Eve! Hello.' Adrian appeared from behind boxes of stock. 'Sorry about the mess... stocktake day. I promise this will be gone before you start.'

'That's okay,' she said as she clambered over another small mountain of yarn. 'Once I've got the shot set up, you carry on. No one ever really knows what goes on behind the camera!' Looking around, despite the chaos, Eve felt she was in paradise.

'It will have to be moved regardless. In case the girls bring their motors.'

'Motors?' she questioned, slightly distracted by the rows upon row of wool balls adorning the walls.

'Sorry,' Claire giggled, 'it's what we call the ladies' happy shopper trolleys. It's how they transport their projects. Some of them still need L-plates!'

By 2pm, the gangway was clear. Right on cue, the bell above the door jangled, as if to announce the arrival of the 'Stitch and Bitches' (their self-proclaimed title. 'Knit and Natter' wasn't really their vibe, apparently).

Even though Claire and Adrian had described the group, Eve didn't really know what to expect. In short, they were a mixed bag. Gladys, Claire said, was the ringleader. She was small and plump with a warm, welcoming face. Beryl was the polar opposite of Gladys in appearance, but they were apparently the best of friends—inseparable, Adrian said. Next, a young woman, around Claire's age, entered the shop; she held the door open for another older lady to enter. As they came into Oddballs, the two of them were deep in conversation.

'I know, but I don't think crochet bikinis are in this year, Doreen. They won't hold up well in the pool,' the younger woman said gently.

So, that's Lissy and Doreen. Claire had talked avidly about them. They'd met at the Stich and Bitch last year and really hit it off. They were now business partners who ran a very successful online shop that sold handmade gifts, which included knitted and crocheted goods. The last person to cause the bell above the door to tinkle was the smallest of the bunch. She gave the group a cute little smile.

That must be Rene!

Gathered around the table, they all looked at Eve excitedly.

Claire cleared her throat. 'Ladies, as promised, we have a special guest joining us for Stitch and Bitch today. Gladys, Beryl, Lissy, Doreen, Rene...please give Eve a warm welcome. She's making a big impact in the online crochet world right now, and it's a privilege that she'd like to talk to us all as part of her project. How exciting is that?!'

There was a chorus of friendly greetings. 'We've heard so much about you, dear. I can't wait to talk to you about wool!' Rene sat down and took her knitting out of her bag.

'I haven't crocheted in years,' said Gladys, settling herself down next to Eve.

'I started a granny square especially for this occasion.' Beryl showed the group a petite square, which had the cutest blend of pink, white and green shades.

'Aw, that's lovely, Beryl.' Eve smiled and Beryl grinned back, blushing slightly.

'I've been watching your progress online,' said Lissy, leaning over. 'Indigo has revived crochet, and you're definitely following in her footsteps. You're doing a great job out there. I'm honoured to be a part of your journey.' Eve blushed.

'Lissy has told me nothing but good things about you, dear. I'm excited, on good recommendation,' added Doreen. 'Plus, I've always loved the lacy look of crochet, especially when it's not too difficult to recreate. I'm open to receiving a crochet tip or two, if there are any going.'

Once all the ladies were seated, their wool out and expectant looks on their faces, Eve felt herself relax. 'Thank you very much for the warm welcome, it's great to be here. Before we begin, I just want to talk you through what we're going to be doing today, as well as a few ground rules I'm obliged to pass on...'

She paused. 'Erm, I don't really think I need to say this, but just in case, no swearing, please.'

Everyone but Eve looked at Rene, who smiled coyly. 'Alright, dearie. I'll be on my best behaviour. Scout's honour.' Rene even saluted.

Eve stifled a laugh. 'Okay, let's get started.' She reached into her bag and retrieved Sim's cardigan. She'd almost finished it. As the women took in the vibrant pink creation, their eyes lit up.

'Oh, that's beautiful!' Beryl gushed, stroking Eve's crochet lovingly.

'Very neat indeed,' Gladys agreed. She adjusted her glasses to see the stitches in finer detail.

'Are you making that for yourself?' asked Rene.

'Oh no, it's for a friend.'

'Well, she's one very lucky friend,' said Doreen.

'Uh-huh,' Eve murmured. She studied the crochet for a moment and let her mind drift to thoughts of Simone. *I wish you'd just answer my calls...*

'Right,' She shook the thoughts from her mind; she had business to attend to. 'Time to knit and knatter!'

'Crochet and chatter!' Beryl added, brandishing her crochet in the air like a mini flag.

'Ooh, Beryl, I like it,' said Eve. 'Let's try and fit it in.' Beryl gave her a thumbs up. 'Okay, I'm going to pop the camera on, but please just forget it's there.'

'I'll get the drinks.' Adrian disappeared upstairs and Claire retreated to the pile of yarn that had spilled into their window display.

'Are you not joining in?' Eve heard Rene whisper to Claire as she passed.

'Not today, I've got loads of counting to do. Plus, Eve looks so at home at the head of the table. You'll all be fabulous, I'm sure. And I'm only back here if you need me.' Claire squeezed

Rene's hand.

'Are you sure you won't join us?' Eve asked.

'Honestly, it's okay. You've got this.' She returned to her stocktaking.

Soon, everyone was settled, each with a woolly project on the go. Adrian served the drinks and conversation flowed. In the first few minutes after Eve pressed 'record', she caught Beryl peering into the screen and Gladys fixing her hair and tugging at her cardigan. Once the subject moved to 'wool politics', however, it felt like they were the only ones there. Eve could barely contain herself. *This is so perfect!*

'It's decision time. Is it a hank or is it skein?' she probed.

'Oh, give me a good old-fashioned ball any day!' Gladys rolled her eyes. 'With hanks, it feels like there's less wool but more faff.' There was a murmur of agreement around the table.

'Oh, I love caking up yarn,' said Beryl, giddiness in voice. 'It's the kind of job I reserve for a Sunday. Very therapeutic.'

Rene let out the cutest little laugh. 'My Sundays are reserved for dirty nappies! That's the day my family come to visit. There's no room for wool when there's a baby around!'

'Online, it says the difference between a hank and skein is that a skein is ready to use, like a ball is. Whereas a hank, you have to wind,' said

Eve. 'There you go, Gladys, you've just got to stick to skeins. Or give your hanks to Beryl to wind.'

'Yes please!' Beryl grinned with glee.

'What about you, Eve? Which do you prefer?' asked Rene.

'Well, until today, I didn't know there was a difference!' she laughed. 'But I must admit, if I use a hank or skein, it's for something special...like a gift or a garment for a special occasion. Therefore, I don't mind putting the effort in to get it ready for use. It's all part of the experience. But, if I'm trying a new skill or I'm making something to wear because my ears are cold, I'll just reach for a ball.'

'And there comes a new dilemma,' said Doreen. 'Do you unwind a ball from the middle or the outside?'

A light-hearted groan travelled around the circle and so began the next debate. In the blink of an eye, their time slot drew to an end. Eve sneaked a glance at the screen and could see that they had over a thousand viewers. *Definitely time to end on a high.*

'Well, ladies, I think that's all we have time for today. Thank you so much.' She turned to the camera. 'And I'll be sure to pass on any questions you lovely lot have for these ladies, so stay tuned for their replies. For now, that's us over and out. Bye!' She stopped the video.

'That's a wrap!' Eve said to the ladies before her.

'Oh, is it? I thought you were making a cardigan,' said Rene innocently. She looked puzzled when everyone laughed.

'It's okay, Rene, I think Eve's got all she needs.' Lissy patted Rene's hand reassuringly.

Eve's grin stretched from ear to ear. 'Ladies, we've got ourselves a live!' She turned her phone round and showed the group what they looked like on screen.

'Ooh!' Beryl clapped her hands together with glee. 'We're living on the internet!'

Eve laughed. 'Yes, you are.'

After collectively answering questions posed in the comments, the ladies finished their drinks and began packing away their projects into their happy shoppers, which Adrian had parked in a neat row behind them.

'Thank you, everyone,' Eve said for the umpteenth time when they were all ready to go, 'you've made this girl very happy.'

'Don't mention it,' said Claire. 'I think the Bitches really enjoyed themselves...didn't you, ladies?' The gaggle nodded happily.

'Most definitely,' said Gladys. 'I rather enjoyed putting the world to rights. We should do it again sometime.'

'Yes, please,' Beryl added.

'You should join us again, dearie, for a proper crochet and chatter...without the camera.' Rene's eyes twinkled.

Eve looked at the expectant faces in front of her. 'Absolutely, I will.'

Chapter Fifteen

Days four and five went by without a hitch. Eve was actually ahead of schedule. She'd already posted her five feed posts (though she planned to do more); her story had never ended; and her third and final live video was all planned out. All that stood between her and victory was a trending hashtag. Over the last two days, she'd shared highlights from her video of the Oddballs' ladies with the hashtag #stitchnbitch; although it had created a rumble in the jungle, it hadn't been enough to throw #justinbieberforever off the top spot.

Trust me to land the same week as Justin Bieber releasing his new album!

Eve sighed. And, despite promising to herself that she wouldn't check Mark's content, she'd seen that he was enjoying a trending hashtag. Granted, it had been a rework of the competition's original: #IBSuperstar. He'd just added the word 'takeover' at the end—but he'd used it on *everything* he'd posted. His approach had worked, largely because he'd reposted every single fan's story that used it, regardless of its content.

#IBSuperstarTakeover. Eve wrinkled her nose as she read it out loud. It was such a cop out. But she (annoyingly) couldn't argue with the

results.

Day six was Saturday—a prime day for audience interaction, Eve had been forewarned. That day, she gave her final live: a crochet masterclass on how to decrease without creating a hole. Indigo's fans loved it...Eve had never seen so many heart-eye emojis given in one video. After it was posted, there was also a flurry of tags from people who wanted to show her what they'd created with their newfound skills.

'Happy to have helped,' Eve responded again and again and again.

***

The final day of takeover week finally rolled around. Eve treated it like any other Sunday and relaxed her pace. She spent most of her time online reminiscing—sharing stories of projects that didn't quite work out as well as those successful makes that looked amazing on completion. Again, Indigo's audience loved it.

'It pays to climb Everest every once in a while,' Eve tweeted at lunchtime, alongside a picture of one of her most complicated blanket designs, all weaving rows and 3D stitch work. That tweet got the most retweets Eve had ever received. She instantly regretted not using her hashtag.

Her last entry on Indigo's socials was a feed

post thanking everyone for their time, inter
actions, and warm welcome into Indigo's world. She posted a picture of Scraggy Ted to accompany it. Scraggy Ted was Eve's first ever amigurumi accomplishment. He'd been a source of entertainment for any young guest to Eve's home and he'd taken a trip around the inside of her mum's washing machine more times than she could remember. Scraggy Ted was the embodiment of why Eve crocheted; why she had such passion for it, and why she continued to pour her heart and soul into her craft. Scraggy Ted symbolised the love and comfort crochet had always given her. He deserved his place on Indigo's grid even if, nowadays, he was threadbare with wonky ears.

Feeling proud of her online activity that week, Eve was just about to turn off the light and get her head down when a notification popped up on her phone. Through sleepy eyes, she saw it was a text from Sharon: *Well done, you did it. #scraggyted is trending!*

Eve unlocked her phone and clicked on the Twitter app. Sure enough, there it was, second from the top of the 'trending' list. Snuggling further under her duvet, she scrolled through the many tweets; they were from around the globe and featured fellow crafters' first attempts at amigurumi...their versions of Eve's 'Scraggy

Ted'. Every piece had its own story, which truly embodied the art.

It was 2am before Eve finally stopped scrolling. She'd lost all track of time, but she'd enjoyed it. Hurriedly, she put her phone down and tried her best to get some sleep, ready for the week ahead.

***

The next day, Eve was getting ready for her shift at the coffee shop when an email pinged, labelled: **URGENT**. It was a message from Sharon that simply read: *Conference Call, NOW.*

Wedging what was left of her toast in her mouth, she turned on her laptop. She absent-mindedly grabbed a glove she'd been hooking for her dad as a thank you present and continued to work on it as she logged into the chat.

She was relieved that she was not the last to enter the call. Mark wasn't online, and neither was his mentor, Hayley.

'Hello, Eve,' Andrew Benson grunted.

'Hi!' Eve said brightly. Her smile fell a little when she noticed how sullen everyone else seemed. At that moment, Hayley's face came on screen, followed by Mark's.

'Brilliant. Welcome, both. Now we're all here, I'll waste no time getting down to business.'

Andrew cleared his throat. 'As some of you are already aware, a rumour has spread online that claims Indigo and Mark are dating, after he was apparently pictured outside Indigo's house.'

Mark looked bemused, but also like he was failing to mask a grin. It made Eve's skin crawl.

'After learning of this rumour earlier this morning, the management team called an emergency meeting. We've decided that the best course of action is just to roll with it. In the few hours it's been circulating, the competition's exposure has rocketed. We've seen a mammoth rise in visits and clicks, and it's not even 9am. Alongside Inga's early departure, we're trending left, right and centre.'

'But won't this give Mark an unfair advantage?' Eve interrupted without thinking. 'People love a romance...won't it persuade them to vote in his favour?'

Andrew laughed. 'You'll just have to work harder, my dear.' She had to stop herself from snapping back. 'Anyway,' he continued briskly, 'we've managed to get you both an interview first thing tomorrow morning on national TV! We're going to tie in yours and Indigo's friendship as well...you know, to get the girl power angle too. So don't stress too much, Eve.'

She almost dropped her crochet. Mark looked

like the cat who'd got the cream, and Indigo looked like she was about to cry.

'Right then. Expect an email from your mentors concerning the angle for your interview, and I'll see you in the morning, bright and early. And, er, from today, I'm officially revoking the 'no close contact with Indigo' ban. We won't be needing *that* anymore! Have a good day, everyone.'

The screen went blank, and she felt sick. *Seriously? Are they actually serious?!*

Chapter Sixteen

'Gooood morning, and welcome back to *Rise and Shine!* I'm so glad you've joined us, because we've got a fabulous exclusive coming up in just a hot second. You won't want to miss it! First, a quick update on the traffic from Lauren.'

Eve had never been one for daytime TV. In fact, she couldn't recall if she'd ever watched a full episode of *Rise and Shine* in her life. One thing was for sure, had she had heard more than a couple of lines from the presenter, Trevor, she would have changed the channel. He was one of the most annoying television personalities she'd ever come across—all teeth and hair and an over-excitedness that lost its charm very quickly, even when the cameras weren't rolling.

A man in a chunky headset waved his hands around. A red light blinked, and they were live.

'So!' Trevor snapped into action, 'I'm sure our viewers will have heard about the online crochet sensation that is Miss Indigo Blue!' There was a roar from the studio audience.

'Overnight, a scandal has come to light surrounding her current Superstar Search competition! Is it all rumours or have we unearthed the truth? Well, I have Indigo here on my sofa today, along with her two remaining contestants. Let's get to the bottom of all of this, live, on *Rise and Shine!* Indigo, hello! How are you?'

'Hi, Trevor.' Indigo smiled at the rapturous applause from the audience. But Eve saw more than they could see. She knew about the façade. Indigo, perched on the edge of the sofa, had crossed her legs at her ankles to stop her feet from trembling. Mark was next to her, and Eve sat on the end. This 'live' interview had been scripted to the nth degree by Indigo's team, and Eve couldn't wait for it to be over.

'Apparently, so a little blue Twitter bird has told me, there's love in the air. Is that right, Indigo?'

Indigo giggled on cue as Mark gave the nearest camera an exaggerated wink.

'Well, that would be telling.' She cast her eyes towards Mark, who waggled his eyebrows suggestively. Eve wanted to retch.

'Oh, come on, Indigo...you can't come here and not give us the juicy gossip!' Trevor gave the camera his best puppy-eyes look. 'Mark, you're the man in question. Can you tell us more?'

'We were trying to keep it under wraps.' Mark placed a hand on Indigo's knee. She couldn't help flinching, but luckily, it appeared to go unnoticed. 'But when the cat's out the bag, what can we do? There's no label on it just yet. But we like each other and, well, we're just seeing where it goes.' Mark moved his arm across the back of Indigo's shoulders; he pulled her in for a kiss on the cheek, which resulted in a ripple of excitement from the audience.

'Woo!' Trevor fanned himself. 'Get a room, guys.'

'And how do you feel about this, Eve?' She was surprised to hear a spatter of applause at her introduction. 'I hear you're currently in the lead in the competition. Does this change anything, in your opinion?'

'Not really,' Eve faked her smile as well as the others. 'During the competition, Indigo and I have got to know each other pretty well too.' Eve and Indigo, as rehearsed, exchanged a look. 'We've become the best of friends. I actually knew that Indigo and Mark were a thing before they did!'

Everyone laughed. It was all going to plan.

'So, in answer to your question, Trevor, I think it's still an even playing field. We'll both come out of this as winners...it just depends on who gets the contract.'

There was another wave of applause from the audience.

'There we have it, ladies and gentlemen, the

truth is out! Love is in the air over the internet, and the competition is still on. Who will win? Will Cupid strike with his arrow, or will girl power win out? Only time will tell! Be sure to keep up to date on the Indigo Blue Superstar Search by following her on social media and have your say on who should be the next crochet superstar. Thank you all for coming on the show today. Give them a round of applause, everybody.'

As the audience applauded once more, the guy with the headset beckoned them all off stage. They headed to the green room where Andrew and Emily were waiting. 'Fantastic job, everyone,' Andrew said quietly. 'We're just waiting for the cars to arrive. Take a quick breather...get a drink or something.'

Not needing to be told twice, people dispersed in different directions. Eve went in search of coffee and, after getting one, went hunting for Indigo. She found her hanging out of an emergency exit, puffing on a cigarette.

'I didn't know you smoked,' said Eve.

'I've just started.' She coughed. 'I can't do this anymore. I'm serious. My life is becoming one big joke.' She stuffed the packet of cigarettes into her tiny handbag and pulled the door shut.

'It's okay.' Eve rubbed her arm. 'I've got a

plan. I just need a bit more time. We've got one more task, right? Do you think you can hold on until then?'

Indigo nodded slowly.

'Ladies, time to go,' Emily's voice carried down the corridor. Eve noticed that Indigo was trembling. She took her hand and almost led her to the green room.

This didn't go unnoticed when they caught up with the others. 'Don't you think that should be me?' Mark smirked.

'He's right,' Emily barked. 'There could be some fans outside. Best keep up appearances.'

Reluctantly, Eve let go of Indigo's hand and Mark took her place. As they left the building, Emily's theory was correct. Phones were flung in their faces, left, right and centre. Fans screamed questions so loudly that you couldn't make out a single voice. Various hands and arms jutted out from all directions. Eve had never felt so disorientated. It seemed like an age before the car door slammed shut and they were away.

Seeing Indigo look so small, shoved up against the window of the taxi, and after taking in Mark's creepy grin as he enjoyed his fifteen minutes of fame, Eve knew it was time. Time to put her plan in motion. All she needed to do was figure out where to start.

Chapter Seventeen

Eve arrived at Blue HQ a week later. It was a hive of activity, with more than double the usual amount of people darting around the place. This was further demonstrated by the number of times she was jostled or bumped into as she walked from reception to the conference room.

'Ah, Eve, I love that you're so eager!' Andrew practically cheered as she entered the room.

'What have they put in his coffee this morning?' she whispered to Indigo after hanging her coat on the designated pegs.

'He's been like it all morning,' Indigo replied, turning her head away from him so he couldn't read her lips. 'He's putting me on edge, if I'm honest.'

A few more people came in who Eve didn't recognise. Before she could ask Indigo about them, Emily appeared, and Andrew clapped his hands to signal he was ready to begin. 'Ladies and gentlemen, may I have your attention, please.' Instantly, the hum of voices in the room stopped. 'Thank you,' he smiled. 'It gives me great pleasure to welcome you all today to the meeting I feel I've been waiting a long, long time for. Exciting times lay ahead, my friends! This is where things start to get HOT!' Eve saw some spittle spray from his mouth with that last bit.

'But first...there's the matter of who won the last task. I must say, watching both of your weeks take shape was a wonderful experience. You did very well, and you completed every element of the task and more. Our vote and the audience's vote once again coincide. Mark... congratulations! You are this task's winner. It's a very worthy win—you went above and beyond our expectations. Can we all give Mark a round of applause?'

'That explains it,' Indigo muttered, just loud enough for Eve to hear over the applause.

'I would love to stand here and give you both constructive feedback. Trust me, I have plenty I wish I could share with you! Sadly, we don't have the time. I will say, though, welcome back to the competition, Mark. It seems that 'helping hand' worked in your favour after all.'

Eve saw Indigo shudder. Mark raised a hand as those around him cheered and whistled.

'But don't worry, Eve,' Andrew reassured her. 'It just means that you'll have to work extra hard on the final task. And I'll now explain what that is. You may have noticed that there are some new faces in the room. Rachel, Lydia, Daniel...come and join me up here.' The three of them got up to stand at his side. One was a tall, thin girl of model proportions, with thick, shiny, dark brown hair that cascaded down her back. The other woman was much smaller; a stumpy girl with thick, black-rimmed glasses and a short, blonde bob. Daniel was a rather muscular male with a buzz cut; he wore an elaborate, fully crocheted rainbow-coloured suit.

'These are our Indigo Blue designers. The team behind all the amazing patterns you've come to love. These three are our best kept secret. As our lovely Indigo's fanbase grew, it pushed the boundaries of what was possible. I mean, how much can the world expect from one girl?'

A polite chuckle rippled through the room, and a few people looked at Indigo for her reaction. She gave an angelical smile that Eve noticed didn't reach her eyes.

'We had to take such steps, to meet the needs of our audience so they didn't lose faith. And thus, our ghost designers were born.' Andrew lifted his hand to his mouth to simulate a whisper. He added, 'Sorry if I've broken the illusion for the new kids. Whilst I'm at it, Santa's not real either.' Another polite laugh, which made Eve shudder. She looked at the faces of those around her; they were all smiling. She couldn't understand how they could be unfazed by the whole façade...the lies, the deceit.

'I thought it only right to invite them along today to set the final task. So, Rachel, Lydia, Daniel...take it away.' He joined Indigo and Eve at the back.

'Hi, guys!' The shorter woman, who Eve presumed to be Lydia, sprang into action. 'For your final task, we wanted to make sure we set you a *real* challenge. The last few tasks in the Superstar search showed you what it's like to be Indigo Blue, but we want to see something more practical. The skill at the root of it all. We want to see you crochet!' Lydia was so excited; she was practically jumping up and down on the spot.

She continued, 'To tie in with the launch of Indigo's fabulous new summer collection, we would like you to design three pieces that can be made using the new yarn. We're only giving you five weeks to complete this task. We'll need all the items to be made by you and for them to be ready to be showcased, with written patterns. Please create one full sized garment and three smaller 'accessory type' pieces.'

Daniel took over, but Eve found it hard to concentrate on his words as she couldn't take her eyes off his suit. 'We'll then host a mini catwalk, here, featuring all the designs. The judges will make their comments before we put your designs through their paces, which means sending your patterns to our dedicated team of testers. This will all be completed in time for the launch party on June 12th. At the launch, we'll host another catwalk for a specially selected audience, made up of Indigo's fans, social media influencers, and various other VIPs. Their votes, together with the judges' votes, and all the votes from the previous tasks, will determine the overall winner…who, along with the main prize of a year's contract with Indigo's team, will also have their patterns included in the new collection release.'

Then it was Rachel's turn. She slinked forward in her figure-hugging dress and said, 'The collection is aptly titled 'Summer Fruits', and it includes a beautiful blend of raspberry, mango, watermelon, pineapple, and kiwi-coloured skeins. You'll get to play around with all five of our fantastic new shades two whole months ahead of their release! The yarn is 100% cotton, and it will make a lightweight and breathable fabric, perfect for summer.' Rachel's voice was a husky whisper. Eve couldn't get over how flirtatious she was, despite talking about such things as raspberry-coloured yarn and breathable fabric.

'So, onto the theme,' Lydia added. 'Do you

have your pen and paper ready? The challenge is to encompass what summer means to you. You have exactly five weeks from today until your initial catwalk. Good luck, and happy hooking!'

'Clearly, she missed her vocation as a kids TV presenter,' Indigo muttered as Andrew walked back up to the front. Eve gave a small snort, which she tried to pass off as a sneeze.

'The pods are now open if you and your mentors wish to use them,' Andrew added. 'However, I must make clear that, after today, your mentors will not be able to give you any more support before your deadline. We don't want them to interfere with your designs, intentionally or otherwise. Best of luck.'

Immediately, Eve felt Sharon's hand on her arm. 'No time like the present,' she said.

***

'Summer...summer...summer....' Eve stared at the starburst she'd drawn as she willed ideas to appear on the notepaper instead.

Eve loved Indigo's new yarn collection. It was squishy and smooth and light, and she knew from her first touch that it would work up a dream. The colours were so exotic! She couldn't wait to get started. What was stopping her was what she should get started on.

It wasn't like she was out of ideas; the floor

around her was littered with crumpled up pieces of paper. They all contained the same summer starburst in the centre with arrows pointing to various woolly ideas. None of them had been bad ideas. But, for this task, Eve felt that a 'not bad idea' would not be good enough.

Why am I bothering? If I'm going to expose everything, what's the point in making perfect pieces for the catwalk?

She quickly batted the thought away. Regardless of her plans for Indigo Blue's team, she didn't want to put a black mark on her own career. Eve still believed she had a future in crochet. An honest, enjoyable one. She therefore wanted to make sure everything she put out into the world, via this competition or otherwise, was the very best it could be.

After the Blue HQ meeting, in a pod with Sharon, they'd broken down the five-week task into manageable chunks. This week was reserved for creative ideas and mood boarding. Eve had enjoyed the last two days scrolling through Pinterest, daydreaming of summer. But now she had to produce some concrete crochet ideas.

In terms of pattern design, Eve wasn't a complete novice. She had, from time to time, rustled up something if she hadn't been able to find what she was looking for elsewhere. But that had involved a lot of guess work or just some pattern modification. She knew her way around a garment, but designing something from scratch was a whole new ball game. And then she had to create a range of sizes…

Brainstorming was not working. She grabbed a pencil and took to doodling women she felt looked 'summer ready'. She drew women in bikinis, women sailing on yachts, women in slinky evening frocks. She drew women on the beach, women dipping their toes in the ocean, and women driving in their convertibles with the top down, the wind in their hair. She even drew a woman sitting on a wall eating an ice cream.

Looking across her drawings, there was one image that stood out as being truly 'summer'. The woman at the beach, complete with sarong and beach bag. That was exactly what Eve imagined when she thought of long summer days. She added a few more details to that doodle and held it up. The light from her bedside lamp gave it a hazy glow.

Perfect. She sighed happily and laid down her pencil. That was enough for now.

***

Next on Eve's agenda was putting more structure to her design. Time seemed to fly by as she tested stitches, swatched tension squares and chose colours. These aspects were within her comfort zone, which meant she was in her element with the colour palette they'd been given. But it wasn't long before she came to the more terrifying part...actually making the items. Before she officially put hook to yarn, she decided to take a break.

She got up to make a coffee and her eyes fell on Simone's pink cardigan by the door. It was neatly folded, which showcased its voluptuous chunky stitches. It was just itching to be worn. She paused in the doorway. She'd completed it over a week ago, and it was all ready to be gifted to Simone. Eve had placed it the corner, almost hiding it away. She reprimanded herself and picked up her phone.

'Pick up, pick up, pick up,' Eve whispered. This was her eleventh attempt to reach her friend. When that call was also denied, she went to make her coffee. *Tonight must be the night.*

Ever since that last meeting at Blue HQ, her stress levels had soared. The working meeting in the pod had been a nightmare; Sharon had just thrown ideas at her and given her no time to think. All the while, Eve had been distracted, as she knew how the competition was going to end. She needed to put her plan in motion. It frightened her a little, the scale of exposure she would likely endure as a result. She couldn't do it alone—she needed help. And all of that was on top of a whole crochet collection she had to design and make.

Yes, now was the time. Coffee in hand, Eve saw that her phone was ringing. Simone's name was on the screen. She almost spilled her drink as she lunged towards it and scrambled for the answer button. 'Hello? Sim?' Eve couldn't quite believe it was her calling.

'Hi,' said a small voice on the other end of line.

There was a pause where neither of the girls knew what to say.

'Oh, Sim,' Eve eventually gushed, 'I've missed you so much. I've tried contacting you loads of times. Jem said you're still really mad at me.' She hadn't planned to go straight in at the deep end—she'd wanted to mention the cardigan first. '*Are* you still mad at me?'

Another pause. Eve bit her lip.

'No,' Sim replied after a moment. 'You just hurt my feelings. I didn't think you loved me...us...anymore. It was like our lives together in our little flat wasn't enough for you...' She trailed off.

Eve sighed. 'I'm so sorry I made you feel that way. It was never my intention. Of course I love you...just as much as I did when we were obnoxious uni students, parading round the shops on student loan day—even if it did mean living off cheap pasta for the rest of the semester.'

Simone gave a small chuckle, which spurred her on. 'Just as much as I did when I held your hair back whilst you were being sick during Freshers' Week. And the Freshers' Week after that, and the one after that...and all the times since. I will always be your sister from another mister, no matter what happens. That hasn't changed...even now, when we haven't been talking. I've still worried and cared about you. It's just that, sometimes, circumstances change, and friendships evolve. This is one of those stages.'

'I know, I know,' Sim conceded. 'I was just being my usual stubborn self. At first, I was mad at you. Like, really mad at you. I thought you were letting fame go to your head. I genuinely thought you were going to let some internet woman ruin our friendship.'

Eve went to interrupt, but she kept talking.

'Then I realised how amazing the opportunity was that you've been given. I've been keeping up with the competition online, and I've seen how well you're getting on. I got really annoyed with myself for not being a good enough friend to you. I've been trying to think of a way to surprise you...'

The line went silent. Eve moved the phone from her ear to check the call was still live. 'Sim, are you still there?'

'And then I got back with Jack, but properly this time. Like, official boyfriend and girlfriend and everything,' she said quickly. 'I knew you'd be annoyed at me, and I was trying to work out a way to tell you...' She trailed off again.

'I'm not annoyed at you. I just never liked the way Jack treated you. But, if he's turned over a new leaf and you're happy, well, I'm happy too.'

Another pause.

'That's good.' Sim paused again then let out a little nervous laugh. 'Gosh, I haven't told anyone this part yet. Well, apart from Jack, obviously...'

'Go on...' Eve held her breath.

'Well, yesterday, I found out that I'm pregnant!'

Eve gasped.

'And I thought you'd be less than impressed. What with Jack being the father. But you called, and now here we are.'

'Oh my god, I wasn't expecting *that*!' Eve squealed. 'Congratulations!' From the moment she'd met Sim, she knew her friend wanted to be a mum more than anything in the world. So much so that she was actually a qualified midwife; she'd gone back to beauty because she couldn't handle the darker side of midwifery. She was a complete softie in many ways, even though she was cold and cutthroat in others. Her heart was definitely in the right place, and Eve wouldn't have changed her for the world.

'Thank you!' Sim squeaked.

'Oh, sod this, I'm coming over,' said Eve. 'We need chocolate and ice cream and belly rubs!'

She heard Sim giggle then there was a gasp. 'Oh no, wait! I've got to tell Jem first. Oh my god! Give me half-an-hour then head over. Eek! I can't wait!'

***

That half-hour passed painfully slowly. After an age, Eve got her things together and headed over to their shared flat. She opened the door to find Sim stood in-front of her, her arms open, ready for a hug. It was just like an airport reunion scene at the end of a rom-com. They both shed a tear.

'You guys,' Jem said, joining their cuddle. They hugged for what felt like an eternity. When they broke apart, Sim got the ice cream, Eve got the spoons, Jem got the chocolate, and they all flopped on the sofa like nothing had changed.

They filled each other in on what had

happened after Eve went to stay at her dad's.

'I'm pretty much exactly where I would have been,' Jem beamed. 'Academically, I've not wasted any time.'

'Good for you, Jem,' Eve said warmly.

Sim nodded. 'Honestly, I've been so proud of her and everything she's achieved. Jem, honey, you've turned your life around. That's no easy feat.'

'Aw, thanks, guys,' Eve could see tears in Jemma's eyes again, but they were definitely happy tears.

'Come on, Eve...surely you've got some exclusive gossip you can share with our budding journo over here,' said Sim.

'Well, funny you should say that. Ladies, I need your help. And I know I've been a rubbish friend of late, and that this is a humongous ask. But you're the best women for the job.'

Simone and Jemma looked at each other.

'Well, now you've built it up like that, there's no question about whether we'll help you!' Jem said, bemused. 'What's the problem?'

Eve took a deep breath. 'Blue HQ is the problem, but I think I've figured out a way to solve it.'

Chapter Eighteen

Eve woke the next morning in her own bed, for the first time in months. Snuggling down under her sheets in the morning sunshine had never felt so heavenly. She let out a long, contented sigh and snuggled down even deeper. She could already hear Sim pottering around the kitchen, singing to her favourite playlist, and the air smelled like warm, buttery toast.

She rolled over a few more times, but eventually prised herself from her bed. She felt so much lighter; being able to tell the girls about all the crazy happenings over the last few months and sharing her concerns about Indigo's future in the industry, had been so therapeutic.

With a spring in her step, Eve got ready for the day. As she did so, something pink caught her eye.

'Dammit.' She snatched it up and raced into the kitchen.

Simone had just sat down to eat her toast when Eve rushed in.

'Sim, here.' Eve handed her the vibrant-pink bundle. 'Please take this before I forget to give it to you again.' She watched her unfold the cardigan. When she did, and she held it up in front of her, Eve saw the emotion etched across her face.

'When we weren't talking, when I missed you, I made you this,' Eve said quietly. 'I hope you like it. It's done in...'

'...that yarn I made you buy.' Sim finished her sentence, her voice breaking. 'Thank you!' She sprang from her seat and wrapped her arms around her friend. 'I absolutely love it!' Sim squeezed her harder as she whispered, 'I'm so glad things are back to normal.'

'Me too.'

As Sim tried on the cardigan, Eve absentmindedly checked her phone. 'Oh, wow, is that the time? I've got to get back to my designs! I'll talk to you later though, okay?'

Sim nodded, returning to her toast.

'And when I've got a more concrete plan, we'll arrange a secret get-together.'

Sim raised an eyebrow.

'I know,' she laughed. 'This is all utter lunacy, but it'll be worth it. I just need to pull some strings first and get everyone I need in on it. Next time I'm over, can you make sure Jack's here, please?'

Sim's expression turned to confusion.

'Of course I want to congratulate him...' Eve began. She avoided Sim's eyes. 'But I could also do with his help.'

'I'm sure he'll be both dumbfounded and

honoured,' she laughed. 'I'll let him know.'

***

The next two weeks of Eve's life were a whirlwind of scheming and crocheting. Her desk at her dad's was divided into two parts—one for her crochet masterpieces, and one for her masterplan, which was currently contained in a notebook aptly entitled: TOP SECRET.

In that fortnight, she managed to crochet all of her accessories and come up with what she deemed a plausible plan of action for her exposure of Blue HQ. Her next step was to find a catwalk model, whilst also rallying her troops ready for battle. When it came to her crochet, Eve was rather specific. The pieces she'd created for her runway moment had been designed to fit her proportions. She'd never made any garment to specifications other than the particular pattern she'd used. Truth be told, she hadn't trusted herself to. What this meant was that she'd crocheted the design to fit her, and just worked out the other sizes using some mathematics. She therefore needed a model that was her shape, size and build. When she thought about it, it really wasn't a problem. Eve suddenly knew exactly who she wanted. Someone who would cause a stir and turn some heads, and someone they couldn't say no to...

As Eve typed out her message, she couldn't help but smile about how everything was coming together. The girl must have lived online, because the moment Eve sent her message, she replied.

Inga: *I'd love to! When do you need me?*

Eve: *Next Friday, please. I've also got another favour to ask you, and a couple of my friends. Would you be able to come over to mine after the catwalk rehearsal?*

Inga: *Sure! I'm intrigued!*

And just like that, all of Eve's wheels were in motion.

Chapter Nineteen

As Inga slipped on Eve's cropped cardigan, she swelled with pride. It had taken one final, humongous push, but she'd made it. She'd completed her full collection that showcased Indigo Blue's new Summer Fruits yarn range. It superseded all of her crochet achievements to date in beauty, neatness and impact.

A gaggle of her nearest and dearest waited for her at the flat, as part of her masterplan.

Five minutes before she was due before the judges, Eve heard murmuring as Indigo slipped in. 'Eve,' she hissed, as she walked the perimeter of the room, pretending to observe Eve's designs from a distance. 'Is everything still on for this afternoon?'

She tried to nod as inconspicuously as she could as she adjusted Inga's headband.

'Okay,' Indigo whispered. 'I'll try and meet you as quickly as I can.' Before Eve could respond, there was an interruption.

'Don't you think this could be considered cheating?' Emily said abruptly, almost appearing out of nowhere.

'Oh, don't worry,' Indigo said as casually as she could muster, 'I'm going to have a sneak peek at my boyfriend's entry in a moment.' It was apparent in her voice how much it pained her to refer to Mark in that manner. She left the room.

'Is everything okay?' Inga whispered as Eve continued to apply a few finishing touches.

'Yes, fine.' Eve double-checked who was in the room. 'I'll explain later,' she said in hushed tones. 'Let's just get this out the way first.' She stepped back and admired her work one more time. 'Perfect! Let's go knock them dead, girl!'

***

'When creating my designs, I wanted to take advantage of the airy, smooth, but strong texture-defining cotton of Indigo's new yarn.' Eve had become quite used to taking centre stage, compared to how nervous she'd been to stick her head above the parapet at the outset of the competition. In the centre of Blue HQ's conference room, a strip of red carpet had been laid out as a makeshift runway for the models to parade upon. The designers had been asked to describe their pieces and the inspiration behind them to the judges, as well as explain their take on the theme of summer.

When Inga strutted down the red carpet, there had been a few surprised faces, but no one said anything. The only thing Eve didn't like was the way Mark kept turning to his mentor and muttering things that made them both grin like Cheshire cats.

'I imagined Indigo's audience ordering from this collection and making something from this range right away, ready for their summer holiday. The inspiration behind my designs under the theme of summer is 'a day at the beach'.' A positive murmur swept across the room.

'From top to toe, I have created...' Eve signalled to Inga to join her, '...a sailor's knot headband. I felt this design captured the essence of nautical life with a feminine flair. Besides looking gorgeous, this piece is also functional; it protects a lady's perfectly styled hairdo from the sea breeze.' Eve was pleased to hear a few appreciative noises from the audience.

'Then there's my cropped cardigan. This is the main garment. It's perfect for evening walks on the beach. I included this cute back panel that features a starburst shape, using more of the yellow, pink and orange-toned yarns to mimic the colours of a sunset, which is when I feel this cardigan would be most appropriate. It also gives it the wow factor, given that this piece is the showstopper of my set.' Again, Eve spotted nods of appreciation from those around her.

'Next up, we have my sarong, which is probably my favourite of the bunch. This is a more intricate design...the lacy pattern would represent the perfect challenge to the more experienced crocheter, as would its asymmetrical shape.' Inga walked up and down to bring the intricacy of the design closer to everyone in the room. 'I think the colour palette really lends itself to this design. It catches the eye and steals attention; it's also flattering for most body shapes, with its elaborate elements.' Further murmurs of appreciation.

'And finally, the perfect holiday accessory: the beach bag, complete with flip flop compartment. I always find, when I take my handbag to the beach, I come back with a mound of sand inside it, which is difficult to get rid of. Whereas, with a crochet bag, you just flip it inside out.' Inga took the bag and gave a demonstration—or at least, she tried to, which made everyone giggle. Eventually, she succeeded. 'On a beach holiday,' Eve continued, 'flip flops are crucial.' She took the bag from Inga and turned it the right way round. 'It's lightweight, roomy, and easy to clean. What's not to love? In summary, the thing I love most about my ensemble is that there's something for everyone. From beginner to expert, I've created designs and pieces that will be loved by all.'

She lowered her notes and looked out to the

audience. For a split-second, all she saw was a sea of stunned faces, but the room quickly erupted into rapturous applause. Indigo was so excited; she gave Eve a standing ovation.

'Okay, Mark, your turn,' Andrew announced, once the applause died down.

Mark stepped forward and cleared his throat. 'As I suspected, Eve created a completely female-orientated collection. Not pointing any fingers, but this is a common occurrence in our world. Although this yarn collection's colour palette did not lend itself to this...' he winked at Indigo, 'I've designed an ensemble for men. Simon, would you come and join us, please?'

Simon appeared from around the curtain and there was an audible gasp from the audience. Eve looked on in awe. He'd done it. Mark had created an entire outfit that any man could happily wear, all with Indigo's yarn.

As Simon walked up and down the carpet, Eve completely understood the vibe Mark had gone for: 'lad's vacay to Ibiza'. Simon wore a string vest, which was a perfect blend of all the colours in Indigo's collection. This was accompanied by a crocheted belt—which was, admittedly, a wicked use of graphghan crochet —and a wristband to match. For Mark's last accessory, Eve had to stifle a laugh.

'Finally, if you're going to wear socks with

sandals, at least make it a fashion statement.' Some people in the audience shared confused looks.

'Correct me if I'm wrong, but I believe I've created the first ever male-targeted Indigo Blue pattern collection, which is my favourite thing about my designs.' Mark concluded his showpiece by taking a bow.

Clapping, Andrew Benson walked to the head of the room. 'Well, well, well...what a treat that has been. Eve, Mark, I think it's fair to say you have both exceeded our expectations. Well done! I'm looking forward to next week.'

***

'So, the plan is simple, really.' Eve stood in front of the group, her TOP SECRET notebook at the ready. Within the space of an hour, they'd all made it to the flat. Even Indigo had been able to escape. And Jack had given Eve a hug when he arrived, which surprised her. *Maybe people can change.*

Claire and Adrian were there. Adrian and Jemma were bonding over video game nonsense, whilst Claire had almost fainted at meeting Indigo Blue in the flesh. Right now, though, everyone's eyes were on Eve.

'At the launch party, there'll be all manner of VIPs and media people there. It's the perfect setting. We'll let the activities go ahead as planned...get the party started, that sort of thing. We'll have the opening speeches, the meal, and the catwalk. Everyone will be relaxed at that point; they'll be letting their hair down. They'll believe it's all done and dusted, that the competition has got them loads of coverage and visibility.' She paused for dramatic effect.

'Then, when they do the announcements and speeches, that's our time. If everything goes according to plan and I win, I'll be expected to make a speech. If I don't win...well, I'll still make a speech, don't worry.' The huddle before her gave her some questioning looks. 'I'll find a way. Trust me. Anyway, during that speech, I'm going to invite Indigo and Jack to the stage. Once you're up there with me, I'll be laying down some home truths, using you both to back up my points. Indigo for the facts...' Indigo gave Eve two thumbs up, '...and Jack for the law stuff.' Jack gave her a nod. 'And this will all be streamed by Jem to social media and her journalist pals. Cue chaos! Our aim then will be to leave the party as quickly as possible, taking Indigo with us. Mission accomplished. Then we'll all meet here for our own after party...for victory drinks and celebrations. We'll just sit back and watch the drama unfold. Any questions?'

There was a flurry of nods and murmurs of

agreement, then Inga raised a hand. 'I've just got one question. If you're the winner of this competition, won't you be burning your bridges? This is the opportunity of a lifetime.'

'It's not a prize anyone should want to win, Inga,' said Indigo sadly. 'Honestly, Eve will do a lot better without it. I promise you all, I'll look after her. This will not go unrewarded.'

'In all honesty, the hardest part of the plan, I believe, will be getting Indigo out of there,' Eve continued. 'If the team get hold of her, they might use her in some way to save face…to make another speech, or a public apology or something. We're going to need a distraction. Sim, Jem—any ideas?'

'We're already on it.' Sim tapped the side of her nose.

1st June 2019 [Scheduled Post]

The importance of staying true to yourself

I've set this post up on a scheduled timer. Hopefully, by the time you read this, everything will be public knowledge.

First of all, I want to apologise to any Indigo Blue fans out there, whose worlds I may have just sent crashing down. That's exactly how I felt when I discovered the truth. It's a biggie, I know. But it's okay—the truth is out now, and I can confirm that…and this has come from a very reliable source…she feels ten times better for it.

I want to affirm the importance of staying true to yourself, and the lies that live behind social media. (Yes, journos, you can quote me.)

I love social media. Its ability to connect people from all over the globe who would otherwise never meet is pretty incredible. However, after getting caught up in this world, as part of the Indigo Blue Superstar Search, I don't like it so much anymore.

Social media has created an idealised world. Something we want to aim for, strive for, dream of. But what we don't realise is the trade-off that occurs to have that 'perfect life'. The lies, the deceit, the greed that comes into play, just to keep people clicking, sharing, liking, following. Did you know, for example, if you don't tweet at least five times a day, you'll be forgotten? True story, I had that said to me recently.

I created my own little corner of the web, Hooks and Kisses, because I enjoyed it. It wasn't meant as a popularity contest, nor was it to make money. It was my hobby; like crochet, it was just something I did. Something I *enjoyed* doing. Don't misunderstand me, there's nothing wrong with making a profit from something you'd be doing anyway. But it becomes a problem when money becomes a greater priority. It should be a bonus, not the reason.

There are so many behind-the-scenes secrets I would love to expose. We need honesty. We need reality. Not this.

Yes, I want slim girls to model my clothes, but I also want curvy girls to do the same. I want girls from all walks of life, with all kinds of amazing stories to tell, to feel good in my designs. And yeah, I want men to get in on the action, too. If that's what they want to wear, let them rock it like the superstars they are.

I want people to review my products because they feel so amazed by them that they have to tell me about it, right away. Not because a company is paying them to do so.

And if I'm going to buy into the personal brand of someone I admire, I want them to have nurtured that idea from creation to birth. To take pride in it, to use it themselves openly and honesty. Not just slap their name on it to help someone else make a sale.

Most importantly, what I want from this blog post is this: I want you to be you. Not the you that you think you should be, or the you that you need to be, or the you that you think you should be to be liked or to fit in. I want you to be who you are, because we're all different, and that's the beauty of the human race.

If you haven't heard the news, check Twitter. I'm sure it's made its way there by now. I hope that you understand my message and that you'll support me through what is bound to be a crazy time.

If I've spoken to your soul through this blog post, tell the world about it—and use the hashtag #TrueBlue. Because if the world can get behind Scraggy Ted, it can get behind this.

Hooks and Kisses
Eve xx

Chapter Twenty

Arriving at the launch party, Eve was hit by a swarm of flashing lights. There were Indigo Blue fans *everywhere*, lining both sides of a familiar-looking piece of red carpet. Eve smiled and posed and tried her best to look as carefree as possible, despite the chants from the crowd about Mark and Indigo's relationship.

She walked into the hotel; inside was a completely different atmosphere. She was offered a flute of champagne, which she took gratefully to calm her nerves. A grand piano was being played and she recognised Cliff Richard's *Summer Holiday*. A beautiful glass chandelier hung from the ceiling. She had to admit, the surroundings were gorgeous—a lot of work had gone into it. She felt a twinge of guilt. *She was going to ruin it all.*

Eve caught sight of Inga waving at her. Happy to spot a friendly face, she made her way over. 'This must have cost thousands!' Inga said when she got close enough.

Eve nodded. The pair clinked their glasses together before they sipped the free champagne. Eve saw that Indigo and Mark were already there. They were locked in deep conversation with Andrew Benson; as she looked closer, she saw they were holding hands.

'The sooner we get this over and done with, the better,' Eve said to Inga.

At that point, Emily appeared with a microphone. 'Ladies and gentlemen, welcome to the launch of the Indigo Blue Summer Fruits Collection. If you'd like to follow me, we shall begin this evening's proceedings.'

She shooed them into the next room where there was a long banqueting table on one side with a seat for every guest. On the other side of the room was a fully illuminated, very professional looking catwalk. Eve saw Inga swallow, hard.

'You'll be fine,' Eve reassured her. 'I'll be up there with you.'

***

'To conclude, I think my favourite thing about my ensemble is that there's something for everyone....' Eve beamed as she spoke into the microphone. Hers and Inga's catwalk moment had gone without a hitch. The pinks, oranges and yellows of the yarn had glimmered under the spotlight, and the intricacies of Eve's designs felt like they'd been delivered in high definition. Inga had even flipped the bag inside and out with little effort at the right points. Eve couldn't have been happier.

They were escorted back to their seats as

Mark began his segment. He also got everything right, and the audience seemed as blown away by his show as they had by hers. *It doesn't matter if you don't win, you'll find another way.* She couldn't lose sight of the real task at hand.

Next, the meal was served, which gave the judges time to mull over their decision before announcing the winner. Eve just picked at her food; she had no appetite. Knowing what was to come made her stomach churn. Soon enough, everyone was in place around the catwalk stage ready for the big announcement. Andrew Benson stood triumphantly on stage.

This is it. Eve quickly checked that everyone was in place. *It's actually happening.*

'Thank you, ladies and gentlemen,' Andrew's voice boomed. 'I now have the great pleasure of announcing the winner of the Indigo Blue Superstar Search.' There was a round of applause. 'A few months ago, three bright-eyed hopefuls joined Indigo's team to win the opportunity of a lifetime. Three became two, and now two must become one. I just wanted to say how proud I am of Mark and Eve. I've watched you positively blossom throughout your time with us. It's truly been a pleasure working with you both. Okay...I don't want to drag this out any longer. The winner is...'

You could have heard a pin drop.

'...Evelyn Jay!'

A second spotlight appeared from nowhere and highlighted Eve in the audience. There was a riot of applause and cheers.

'Come and join me, Eve! I'm sure you'd like to say a few words.'

Eve felt people patting her on the back as she was guided onto the stage. Her legs wobbly, she wanted to escape everyone's eyes on her. *Oh god, here goes.* With trembling hands, Eve took the microphone from Andrew.

For a split second, she froze, inwardly debating if she could do it. Could she—should she—selflessly throw this all away for someone else? Eve searched the crowd for Indigo, who looked back at her adoringly, her eyes twinkling. Next to her was a disgruntled Mark, leering over her shoulder.

'Thank you, Andrew,' she acknowledged. Turning to the sea of faces, she said, 'Thank you all for picking me as your 'Superstar'. I'm deeply touched.' This was *her* moment, in so many ways. 'Throughout this competition, I have indeed learned a lot, and I'm so glad that all my hard work and best efforts have paid off. In fact, my speech is about the things I've learned.'

She focused on one face in the crowd.

'Indigo? Could you join me on stage. please?' Eve paused to allow Indigo, closely followed by Jack, to come on stage. 'Everything you've seen from me during this competition has been my own doing. My designs, my videos, my ideas, my opinions. It's all real, all genuine. However, I learned quite early on in this competition that this wasn't so true for Indigo and her team. Was it?' Eve passed her the microphone, and she took it confidently.

'No.' Indigo sighed but she held her head high. 'Over the past four years my online presence has become a spider's web of fabricated lies. It's all fake! Right down to this stupid bloody wig!' There was a gasp from the audience as Indigo removed her perfectly curled vivid-blue wig to reveal her rather bedraggled, mousy-brown pixie cut underneath. But the shocked sounds didn't stop her. 'I no longer personally test every product I review...I pretty much get paid to breathe, and I've never designed a crochet pattern in my life!' Eve saw Andrew Benson's face turn cherry red as he silently screamed at the people around him to do something.

Indigo ploughed on, 'I am not in love with Mark. I do not sit in my bedroom anymore and crochet—though I wish I did—and I don't want to be the centre of attention anymore! I QUIT!

You can take this as my verbal resignation.'

More shocked gasps. People looked at each other with a mix of disbelief and unease on their faces, unsure if what was happening was real or some kind of publicity stunt.

Eve spotted Emily marching up to the stage and a bolt of panic shot down her spine. They needed to wrap this up and flee, but how? On cue, there was a wail of pain from the audience, which even saw Emily stop in her tracks. Heads turned to the source of the noise. Perfectly placed, in the middle of the room, was Simone, bent double, breathing heavily.

Eve quickly took the mic from Indigo. 'Thank you for listening,' she added, before passing it to Jack and grabbing Indigo's hand. They caught the first few lines of Jack's speech on human rights in the workplace before they left the room.

'Please, everybody, stand back. Pregnant lady here,' Jem called out, trying to clear a space around Sim.

The confusion allowed the women to slip out seamlessly. They even lost sight of Emily in the commotion.

With Rosie on one arm, Jem on the other, Sim was slowly led through the crowd to the main exit. Eve and Indigo headed for one of the side fire exits. As they turned a corner, they came face to face with Mark, who blocked the doorway.

His rage was visible. 'You've ruined it. You've ruined *everything*. I could have had a career; I could have made millions! Now you've ruined it for me, *forever*.' Mark grabbed the top of Indigo's arm tightly. 'I can't let you go. You've got to go back out there. Take it all back. Tell them you didn't mean it…say it was a joke or a publicity stunt. Say anything! You can't do this to me, it isn't fair! What did I ever do to you?!'

Without thinking, Indigo reached up with her other hand and slapped Mark square round the face, stunning him into silence.

'Wake up!' Indigo screamed. 'I haven't ruined anything. In fact, I've saved you, you idiot!' She broke free from his grasp and pushed past him.

'These people are vile!' she shouted as she pushed open the fire door. 'They're money hungry liars. They'll put you through anything to make a couple of pennies. You're better off without them!'

Eve followed in her wake. She couldn't help but glance back; Mark appeared absolutely crushed—his dreams in tatters. Any guilt she was holding onto disappeared completely once she'd caught up with Indigo and took in the huge grin on her face.

'We did it!' Her relief was practically tangible.

She gave Eve's hand a squeeze. 'Thank you!'

They found Adrian and Claire waiting where they said they would be, in their little Nissan Micra. The exhaust rattled as the engine purred. 'I believe someone ordered a getaway car.' Adrian grinned at them both as they climbed inside.

'Sorry it's not a limousine like you're used to, Indigo,' Claire added, a little colour in her cheeks.

Indigo laughed as she buckled herself in. 'Right now, this is absolutely perfect. Thank you. Thank you, all of you.' Indigo closed her eyes as they drove away—the epitome of peace, despite her messy hair and rosy cheeks.

***

In the safety of the flat, with all of her friends there too, Eve locked and bolted the door before flopping down on the sofa.

They all gave a cheer.

'Well done, babe! You were amazing,' gushed Sim.

'Thank you so much. I would have never been able to do this without you,' said Indigo.

'You're trending on Twitter!' Jem exclaimed, waving her phone around. 'And look at this bad ass shot they got of you!'

Looking at her screen, Eve giggled. It must have been taken by one of the content creators sitting close to the stage, because the detail was perfect. It was an action shot of Indigo and Eve exiting, stage left. It could have been used as the poster for an action movie, given her look of steely determination.

'Now you've exposed one of the biggest names in the industry, what are you going to do?' asked Inga.

'Yeah... Somehow, I don't think your winning contract is valid anymore,' Jem added.

'It's okay.' Eve smiled at Indigo. 'I'll be just fine.' She picked up the drink Sim had just poured for her. 'Let's all raise a glass to truth and honesty, no matter the cost.'

Indigo smiled. 'To invaluable friendships, new and old.'

Eve noticed Jem and Inga cosied up on the sofa, chatting away like they'd known each other for years. 'And to bright futures,' she concluded. 'Cheers!' She raised her glass of bubbly.

'Cheers!' everyone chimed back, as they raised their own glasses.

24th July 2019

What the future holds for Hooks and Kisses...

Hi, everyone,

So...after the drama of the Indigo Blue Superstar Search (for those of you who have no idea what I'm talking about, you can read all about it online here), I wanted to let you all know what's next for me in the world of wool.

Following recent events, I took some time out to stop and reflect. After all the craziness, I wanted to reconnect with my friends and to get to know my new ones better!

I've officially moved back into my flat with my best friends. That said, this won't be for too long, as my beautiful friend Simone is pregnant! Can you believe it?! I'm so excited. I'm going to crochet all the clothes the baby will ever need! Simone plans to move out, and at that point, me and my other friend and flatmate, Jemma, have agreed that I can convert part of the living room into an office space (I made the trade-off that Simone's bedroom can become Jemma's gaming den!). How cool is that?

So, onto why I would need an office. I'm pleased to announce that, out of the ashes of that competition, I plan to rise like a phoenix!

I have an agent. You might know her, actually. She's about five-foot-two, she *used* to have bright blue hair, and her first name is Indigo.

Indie may have retired from the limelight, but she's putting all of her amazing knowledge and experience to good use. I'm so glad she's my agent, because she's also been my rock and my mentor through this crazy crochet journey! I simply cannot wait. Expect fantastic things from us, such as my yarn collection debut and new patterns winging their way to you very soon!

In getting to know some new friends, I've also gained my first stockists: *Oddballs*, in Rosworth! The owners, Adrian and Claire, have been a huge support to me both during and after the competition, and I'm very proud to say I'll be working alongside them very closely. Watch this space!

I also want to take this opportunity to set the record straight (because I've seen a few rumours online). From my point of view, there is absolutely no bad blood between me and fellow Superstar contestant Mark Roberts. I honestly hope that his career goes well, and that his male-orientated crochet designs become a huge success. Maybe our paths will cross again someday.

All that's left for me to say is thank you. Honestly, I wish I could hug every single one of you out there who has supported me through everything and who is still here for me, despite all the drama. You mean the world to me, and I promise you, with the future I have planned for this platform, your loyalty and support will most definitely be rewarded.

Hooks and Kisses
Eve xx

Views: 40.7k
Likes: 3,928
Comments have been disabled on this post by admin.

Acknowledgements

Username handles in these acknowledgments are taken from a variety of social media platforms. However, if you find yourself stumbling across any of these amazing people, I truly suggest you give them a like, a follow, and a share. They are all wonderful stars in my galaxy, and I wouldn't be doing this without them.

#followfriday
@binglebangbang
@thewritinghall
@janetheknit
@brianisms
@bobby_puplife
@ellessseprime
@alittlecreatorillustration

P.S: I think I need to create a TikTok account for my hamster...